The Pot Thief Who Studied Calvin

The Pot Thief Who Studied Calvin

A Pot Thief Mystery

J. MICHAEL ORENDUFF

OPEN ROAD

INTEGRATED MEDIA

NEW YORK

Copyright © 2024 by J. Michael Orenduff

ISBN: 978-1-5040-8680-6

Published in 2025 by Open Road Integrated Media, Inc.
180 Maiden Lane
New York, NY 10038
www.openroadmedia.com

Dedcations

Henry Dennis Babers

Dennis and I were on Naval Reserve Officers Training Corp scholarships at the University of Mississippi. He took some ribbing from the other cadets (myself included, I am ashamed to admit) because he was not "cool."

At the end of one of our summer training periods at Quantico, midshipmen from all over the nation were required to rate their fellow cadets as first, second, third, or fourth quartile. I was called in by the commander in charge of the training, who told me Babers had been placed in the fourth quartile by many of the cadets. He asked me, in a tone that suggested I had erred, why I had rated him higher. When I said maybe it was because I had seen Babers in more situations than the others had because Babers and I were at the same university, the commander accused me of ranking Babers too high merely because we were classmates.

"No, sir," I said. "I rated him to the best of my ability."

"Perhaps you don't have much of that ability."

"Perhaps I don't. I'm nineteen years old. I'm in a program that is supposed to turn me into a leader of men. If I had all the skills necessary for that, I wouldn't need this training program."

"Would you follow Babers into battle?"

"Absolutely."

Dennis graduated in 1966 and was commissioned in the US Marine Corps. He died in Quảng Tri Province, Vietnam, on September 18, 1967, while serving with the Third Marine Division.

He was not fourth quartile. He was a leader of men.

I was honorably discharged from the navy the year Dennis died. During my service, I was never in danger. Life is not fair.

In the story that follows, the fictional Dennis dies in Iraq rather than Vietnam because it fits the time line of the book.

Jim Hoffsis

I met Jim Hoffsis in 2008, when my first book was published. I'd attended the University of New Mexico, taught with my wife at Jemez Springs and at the Pueblo, and served as president of New Mexico State University. We looked forward to returning to New Mexico for a signing tour. Normally, bookstores won't host signings for unknown authors whose books are from small publishers. But my book had a blurb from then-Governor Bill Richardson, and that got me into the stores—chains such as Borders, Waldenbooks, and Barnes & Noble, and independents such as Bookworks in Albuquerque, COAS in Las Cruces, Imaginary Books in Cloudcroft, Tome on the Range in Las Vegas, The Mystery Store in Chama, and a bunch of others.

Sales were miserable. We spent the last day in Old Town. I spotted Treasure House Books & Gifts. I didn't know it existed. I asked the man behind the counter if he would take a book on consignment. He looked skeptical. Then he looked at the book. "I've been trying to contact you. A lot of our customers are looking for your book." Turns out the book had been reviewed in the *Albuquerque Journal*. "I'll take ten copies," he said, "and I want you to sign them all."

Jim and his son John had been running the store for years, and they made a great tag team. John would keep track of things, and Jim would chat with the browsers, although each could do both when called upon.

We were headed home when I got a call asking me to sign and mail twenty-four more copies to Treasure House ASAP. I couldn't believe my good fortune. I'd travelled all over New Mexico and sold about five copies per bookstore, and this little place in Old Town had sold ten and was looking for two dozen more!

That first book won the New Mexico Book of the Year Award, no doubt in large part because Treasure House sold so many copies. I started getting emails from people who had bought my book. Jim and his son John were recommending it to tourists who wanted to read something set there, in Old Town, New Mexico. Since the tourists were in Old Town and the series is set there, they were buying the book.

When I did the launch signing for the second book at Treasure House, the line of people stretched out to the sidewalk. Same with the third book, which won the Lefty for best humorous mystery of the year. I eventually became a best-selling author, and I owe that to Jim and John Hoffsis.

Borders, Hastings, and Waldenbooks all went bankrupt. Imaginary Books, The Mystery Store, and a lot of little independent bookstores were shuttered. But Treasure House is still operating in a store that's probably smaller than your living room.

Sadly, it is now operating without Jim Hoffsis, who died October 8, 2021. Jim read every one of my books from cover to cover. He gave me advice about what customers liked. He even gave me writing advice—and advice about life, which he knew well because he enjoyed ninety-three years of it.

Jim loved his family and his country. He was a veteran, and he participated in the Bataan Memorial Death March at White Sands Missile Range with John for many years and was often the oldest person to complete the course. He loved hosting the Navajo World War II code talkers at Treasure House. There were four hundred Navajos who served in the war in the Pacific. Twenty-nine were killed in action. All the code talkers received congressional medals. I believe four of them are still alive.

Knowing how fervently Jim recommended my books to everyone, I suspect a lot of people in heaven are reading Pot Thief books.

The Pot Thief
Who Studied
Calvin

1

It was my third trip to the morgue. Even though a year or two had passed between visits, this body looked just like the first two I'd seen.

Dead.

It's a look you don't forget.

I assumed the deceased would be one of the half-dozen or so people connected to a strange little piece of pottery I had that was evidently worth killing for.

But it wasn't any of those people. It was someone I'd seen only in passing. Someone who, so far as I knew, had no connection to me or to the pot.

Which prompted me to ask Detective Whit Fletcher of the Albuquerque Police Department why he'd dragged me down to the morgue to make an ID I couldn't make.

Then he pulled a torn piece of paper out of his pocket and showed it to me.

And my theory about the little pot and who wanted it and why they wanted it went up in smoke.

2

One month earlier

It was a slow day at Barnegat Books, but then most of them are. Antiquarian booksellers, after all, do not dream of retiring to the slow and simple life. They are already living it."
    —*The Burglar who Studied Spinoza* by Lawrence Block

I remembered that quote from a book Susannah insisted I read a few years back.

Susannah is a murder mystery fan.

I am not.

But when Susannah insists I do something, I usually end up doing it. She has a lot more gumption than I do, probably because she grew up on a ranch and had to get up at sunrise to shear sheep, castrate calves, and whatever else it is they do on ranches.

She also has a bit of guile which is why she picked a book with Spinoza in the title. She knows I'm interested in obscure thinkers like Pythagoras, Ptolemy, and Spinoza.

Turns out Spinoza is little more than a footnote in the book. The main character is a bookseller named Bernie Rhodenbarr.

I identified somewhat with Bernie. Like him, I'm a merchant. Like him, I lead the slow life. I sell pottery instead of books, and

I thought that gave me an advantage over Bernie because e-books could undermine his sales of real books with paper pages.

I didn't have to worry about anything like that because there's no such thing as an e-pot.

Or so I thought. Then my nephew Tristan came into my shop in Albuquerque's Old Town and placed a beautiful little pot on my counter.

Tristan is a student at my alma mater, the University of New Mexico, known locally as UNM. He studies computer science and has never shown any interest in pots, so I was surprised he brought me one.

"Look what I made," he said. "What do you think of it?"

"It's beautiful. I like the curvy line decorations. I've never seen anything like it." I picked it up for a closer look. "It isn't glazed."

"It isn't glazed because I don't have a kiln."

"You also don't have a wheel, so how did you throw a pot?"

He gave me that big dopey smile of his and said, "I didn't throw it. I made it using a 3-D printer."

I stared at him blankly.

His smile widened. "You don't know what a 3-D printer is, do you?"

"Sounds like something that prints the letters in such a way that if you look at the page using those old cardboard glasses with a red lens over one eye and a green lens over the other, the text will seem to jump off the page."

Now it was his turn to give me a blank stare. He prefers TV to movie theaters, so he's never seen the new 3-D films and is way too young to know about the old 3-D movies.

"A 3-D printer doesn't print books," he explained. "It prints three-dimensional objects."

"If it doesn't print books, why is it called a printer?"

He shrugged. "I guess because it has a stylus that moves around. But instead of moving on a two-dimensional plane, it can move in three dimensions. And that's how this pot was made. The stylus was set up to emit clay rather than ink, and it can keep piling up thin layers of clay to form a pot."

"So you guide it around like a spray gun shooting out clay until you have a pot?"

"No. It can operate in several ways. The one I used sets the printer to run its stylus over the surface of an object you want to copy. The movements of the stylus are stored in the printer's memory. Then you have it follow the pattern of the object it now has in its memory, but this time it's laying down soft clay as it goes, so it makes an exact duplicate of the object it traced."

"So it's like when you get a key made, and they use that machine with one arm that follows the pattern of your old key and another arm that grinds that same pattern into a blank key?"

"Right. Except instead of grinding down something to a certain shape, the 3-D printer creates that shape by expelling clay. Like sculpting by addition instead of subtraction. Of course you have to do a bit of programming to get it all to work."

Sounded weird. And sort of scary. "You own one of those things?"

He shook his head. "Way too expensive. A guy named Nomolos has one. He's not tech savvy, so he hired me to program it for him and get it to make some duplicates of a pot he has. After we struck a deal over the phone, he sent a guy over to my place with the printer, a big bag of semi-liquid clay, a few sheets of two-thousand-grit sandpaper, the pot he wanted duplicated, and four crisp hundred-dollar bills. It took me three hours to set up the machine, write the program, and trace the pot. But it took less than thirty minutes to make nine duplicates. The machine is really fast. I figure I made about a hundred dollars an hour for this job."

Tristan's dark hair hangs down in short loose ringlets. I used to describe him as appearing to have a layer of baby fat even though he was in his twenties. But he's now in his thirties, and the layer is still here, so there must be another explanation, and I suspect it's the *chicharrones* and *cerveza* he lives on.

He doesn't have what you'd call "leading man" looks, but girls find him irresistible.

Unfortunately, girls have generally been resisting me without difficulty since I went through puberty thirty-eight years ago.

The major exception is my fiancé, Sharice Clarke, with whom I have been living for the past couple of years. We dated for a while before I moved into her downtown loft, and we are now expecting a child, much to the chagrin of her father, Collin Clarke of Montreal, Quebec, who explained to me in black and white that he opposes our forthcoming marriage. Of course "black and white" is a metaphor for "in print"—something you can count on. But in this case, it is also a *double entendre* because her ancestors came from Africa and mine from Eastern Europe.

I'm temporarily out of the condo and sleeping alone again in the little living area behind my pottery store because Mr. Clarke is staying with Sharice in the condo. She invited him to visit in order to convince him to give her hand in marriage. I suspect the reason he came is because he hopes to convince her to jilt me.

I'm not worried about it. I know how committed she and I are to each other.

I was happy Tristan earned some easy money making the pots. I frequently give him money which he describes as loans. He keeps a running total because he plans to pay me back after he graduates and gets a full-time job, neither of which event is visible on the time line horizon.

I don't keep count because I don't expect to be repaid. However, I was a bit low on funds—remember I mentioned that selling pots is not high volume—so I was happy he was not in immediate need of another loan. But summer school tuition was looming.

He calls me Uncle Hubie, which is good because I think of him as my nephew, but he's actually the grandson of my mother's sister, which makes him a first cousin once removed.

But not very far removed. His apartment in a student ghetto near the corner of Maple Street and Lead Avenue is less than three miles from my building in Old Town, Albuquerque.

Although Old Town, the original center of Albuquerque, has become somewhat twee, I've tried to keep my little piece of it looking like it did when Don Fernando Maria Arajuez Aragon built it in 1680.

When I acquired the east third of the building, it came with a several-centuries-long backlog of deferred maintenance. My

remodel of the interior included removing everything down to the
original adobe bricks and covering them with adobe plaster. It was
like making the largest pot in the world, and working on it from
the inside. I included two expansion joints, but they aren't there for
expansion purposes. They are the edges of a small door that swings
open when I turn and press the wall sconce. Behind the little door
is a hiding place for pots and cash. The former because I don't
technically own them, and the latter because it wasn't reported to
the IRS.

The exterior of the building has no signs on its brown adobe.
It had no signs at all until Susannah convinced me to let her art
history classmates put one on the glass front door. The logo they
designed has two stylized hands, one reaching up out of the ground,
the other one down from above. The two hands wind around each
other in a double helix to form a pot. I see it as symbolic of the
ancient potters giving me their work to sell because they want it to
be seen and admired.

On the glass door, I could see the name of my shop, Spirits in
Clay, under the logo. It looked like this: ʏɒlƆ ni ꙅƚiⁱɿiqꙅ

Well, what did you expect? I was looking at it from inside.

Little did I know that the mirror image I saw would be one of
the clues related to a murder.

The main reason I didn't see it as a clue at that point was no one
had been murdered. At least not that I knew about. That would
happen later.

I asked Tristan why he made nine copies.

"Actually, Nomolos wanted only eight, but I made nine because
I figured you'd like to see one."

The number of pots also turned out to be a clue. I suppose if it
had been one of Susannah's murder mysteries and I were a clever
person like Bernie Rhodenbarr, Junior Bender, or Miss Marple, I
would have solved the murder before it was committed, but I'm
not and I didn't.

"Does he plan to glaze the pots?" I asked.

"He didn't say."

I picked up the pot to get a closer look. "Why can't I see the
layers of clay?"

"The machine is extremely precise. It has an IT12 rating."

"In English?"

"The International Standards Organization (ISO) has a system of tolerance grades. IT numbers rate tolerance."

I said, "Iran and North Korea must have low ITs," but it got a smile instead of a laugh.

"It is how much variance there is between the object and the copy. The twelve rating is excellent," he explained. "It means the surfaces cannot vary more than one tenth of a millimeter. You know how small that is because you're a numbers geek."

I did the math. "Slightly less than four one-thousandths of an inch."

"Got an example?"

"The thickness of a typical piece of writing paper."

"Sounds about right," he said. "When I ran my hand over the pots after they dried, they felt just like unglazed clay, rough but not layered. What gave away the layering was not the feel, but the appearance. You could see a few fine hairlines between layers. Nomolos' instructions included sanding the new pots lightly with the two-thousand-grit sandpaper he brought. Just a light rub and the lines were gone. Didn't want to sand away the design feature."

I wondered why Nomolos wanted the pots. Unglazed pottery breaks too easily to be useful. I suppose you could put flowers in them, but they'd have to be clover blossoms because the pot was too small to hold even one ordinary daisy. It was about the size of a cappuccino cup, so you could also drink coffee from it. But because the pot was unglazed, the coffee would partially penetrate the clay, and after a while, water drunk out of the pot would have a slight coffee flavor. That fact about unglazed clay also played a part in figuring out what happened to the guy in the morgue.

I wondered if 3-D printed pots would undermine sales of pots made on wheels, which is a much slower process. Nomolos had paid Tristan about $50 a pot. But that included setting up and programming the machine.

The actual making of the nine copies took only half an hour. So that's eighteen copies an hour. If you paid someone $18 an hour to make them, that's a dollar in labor per pot. Clay is cheap and the pots were small. So call it a dollar's worth of clay per pot.

You'd have $2 labor and material invested in a pot you can easily sell for $15. So your 3-D printer is making you over $200 profit every hour while you're taking a walk or reading a book—preferably not a murder mystery.

As you may have noticed in the title of the book Susannah made me read, Bernie is a burglar. So in his world, he could be breaking into someone's house and stealing money even faster than his 3-D printer was making it.

Which brings me to a confession. Both of us being merchants in a slow-paced trade is not the only thing Bernie and I have in common.

I, too, am a thief.

Now Bernie is a forthright guy. He admits he's a burglar and admits it's a character flaw, but he states right up front that he keeps doing it because he loves it.

My being a thief is only a technicality. The Federal Government—specifically the Bureau of Land Management—classifies me as one. That's why some of my pots are in my secret compartment. But those pots are not stolen; they are rescued.

I dig up pots made by the original inhabitants of New Mexico. I do all my digging on public land. If I find a piece of turquoise, I can legally keep it. If I find a rusty piece of barbed wire from the 19th century, I can legally keep it.

But if I find a thousand-year-old clay pot and keep it, I'm breaking the Archaeological Resources Protection Act (ARPA). Instead of keeping it, I'm required to turn it over to the BLM who will put it under the protection of a professional archaeologist for study.

There are three problems with that system.

First, there are so many "archaeological resources" dug up that most of them end up in storerooms and will never be studied because there aren't enough archaeologists to do so.

Second, I know more about those pots than any archaeologist could possibly learn because I know exactly where they were found and what other objects were around them. This is a concept archaeologists refer to as *provenience* or *the multidimensional original place.*

The third problem is the one I most care about. The women who made those pots don't want them in storage rooms. And they don't want them to remain forever buried in the desert. They are proud of their work. They want it to be seen and appreciated.

How do I know that? I'm also a potter. When my hands are in clay, the ancient potters communicate with me.

3

You are a thief!"

I was happy the counter was between us. He looked angry enough to strike me. Collin Clarke is old, but he is tall, wiry and fit.

I am short and have never been described as fit.

"I am not a thief," I replied. "Digging up pots was legal in this country for over two hundred years until Congress passed the Archaeological Resources Protection Act of 1979. People who dug up pots back then were called treasure hunters and were generally admired, sort of like real-life Indiana Joneses. But the law is ridiculous because no one owns those pots, so digging them up is not thievery."

"Your Congress thinks otherwise."

"Congress is not infallible."

"They make the laws."

"Yes," I replied, "and they passed the Fugitive Slave Law requiring that all escaped slaves, upon capture, be returned to their masters and that officials and citizens of free states had to cooperate. But Ellen White, whom your church considers a prophet, taught that Adventists should disregard the Fugitive Slave Act just like I disregard the Archaeological Resources Protection Act."

I knew about Ellen White because I had started reading about the Seventh-day Adventist Church when Sharice told me her father was a member of that denomination.

"You dare to lecture me on my own faith?"

I marveled that he could speak so forcefully with his jaw clinched so tightly.

My jaw was relaxed because I was trying to remain calm. "I'm not lecturing; I'm stating a fact. The Fugitive Slave Acts were repealed, and I hope the Archaeological Resources Protection Act will meet the same fate. But the issue is moot. I know I'm not a thief. And, more importantly, Sharice knows I'm not a thief."

"You two are making a grave mistake. A marriage commitment is to God as well as to the spouse, and should be entered into only between a man and a woman who share a common faith."

"Sharice and I do share a common faith. We are both Anglicans."

"She was raised as a Seventh-day Adventist."

"You *tried* to raise her as a Seventh-day Adventist. But she says her mother raised her as an Anglican."

His countenance softened slightly, and he seemed to shrink a bit. "Is there nothing that girl won't share with you?"

"She and I are in love, Mr. Clarke. We share everything. She has told me that you and her mother had a perfect marriage. I feel the same way about my parents. Sharice and I will also have a perfect marriage."

Okay, so Sharice and I are cockeyed optimists.

He shook his head. "I don't want my daughter to endure the problems faced by a mixed-race marriage. She will be much better off marrying someone of the same race."

"Sharice and I *are* of the same race—the human race."

"You are an idealistic dreamer."

"Thank you."

"I didn't mean it as a compliment."

"I know that. But it is one. Idealistic dreamers make the world a better place."

"You have studied my faith to use it against me."

"No. I have studied your faith because you are soon to be my father-in-law."

"I do not seek that role."

"I know. But your daughter wants that role for you. And you love her too much to stand in her way."

He was silent for a moment.

"I will pray about it," he said.

"Do so soon," I replied. "Babies don't wait."

He turned and walked out.

4

After Mr. Clarke left, I tried to decide whether his visit would have any effect on the odds that he would in fact participate in the upcoming marriage ceremony.

I figured it must have raised them a bit since the odds after the first time we met—an extremely unpleasant exchange also in my shop—were zero.

There were no customers after he left. Which is almost the way I like it. Gives me time to read.

When I checked out the book about the Seventh-day Adventist Church to read up on Mr. Clarke's denomination, I'd noticed another interesting book in the religion and philosophy section—*Sky Determines: An Interpretation of the Southwest* by Ross Calvin. I remembered my father had a dog-eared copy of that book on his bookshelf. I wondered if Ross Calvin belonged among my favorite obscure thinkers like Pythagoras, Ptolemy, and Spinoza.

So I checked out Calvin's *Sky Determines* and also a biography of Calvin: *Ross Calvin, Interpreter of the American Southwest* by Ron Hamm.

I decided to read the biography first and learned that Ross Calvin grew up on his family's farm in Illinois and was fascinated by wild animals and plants. But it wasn't the local fauna and flora that brought him to New Mexico. Like many people who came to New Mexico in the early 1900s, he came because he believed the climate would heal his respiratory problem. Evidently it did because he lived to be eighty. Before coming west, he had earned a PhD at Harvard. The subject he studied was philology. I read the dictionary, and even I had to look it up. It's the study of the history of languages.

He later entered a New York City seminary and studied theology. At least I know what that is. He came to Silver City in 1927 to take the post of rector of the local Episcopal Church, The Church of the Good Shepherd.

I imagine he was the only person in Silver City with a doctorate from Harvard. Or from any other university. Indeed, he may have been the only person with a PhD in philology west of the Mississippi River.

Like John Calvin, a key figure in the reformation in the 16th century, Ross Calvin was dedicated to the philosophy of predestination which is part of the doctrine of the Episcopal Church in which he was a priest. Predestination is the theory that God has chosen which people will be saved, and if you are not among the chosen, there is nothing you can do to change your ultimate fate.

Seems rather harsh, which is probably why Lutherans and many other Protestant denominations believe that salvation is not predestined but is open to all who do and believe what they are supposed to do and believe. I've always found it odd that so few churches agree on these things and argue over whether you should be baptized by dunking or sprinkling and whether the Sabbath begins Friday night or Saturday night.

Sharice and I are Anglicans (that's what she calls it because she's Canadian; we Americans call it Episcopal), and even though predestination has long been the official position of the Anglican Church, most members today do not embrace that doctrine.

Ross Calvin had a unique twist regarding predestination or determinism and New Mexico; namely that almost everything in New Mexico is determined, not by God directly, but in part indirectly by the sky. Hence the title of his major book, *Sky Determines*. He argues that almost everything in this part of the world is a result of the sky and its water (or lack thereof) and heat. I wondered however if *sky* was also a sort of poetic reference to God.

I read until about 4:30 p.m. then closed up and walked, book in hand, over to Dos Hermanas Tortilleria where Susannah and I usually meet for margaritas when she doesn't have a date. Sharice usually joins us except when she's working late. Or her father is in town.

The book I read about Seventh-day Adventists said, "Adventists do not drink alcohol. Adventists view their bodies as a temple of God."

Sharice enjoys alcohol in moderation, and so far as I can tell, it has had no ill effects on her body which is as close to a temple of God as anything I ever expect to encounter.

She does have a small scar where her left breast used to be. I see it as a badge of courage and as the only thing that reveals her to be human rather than a goddess.

Susannah hadn't arrived, so I read some more while I waited, then put the book in my pocket when Susannah entered. Angie also saw her, came to our table, and placed two margaritas on it. "With salt for you, Mr. Schuze, and without for you, Miss Inchaustigui. And here's the pico de gallo and chips."

Angie grew up in a formal Hispano family. Susannah and I have given up trying to get her to use our first names. But she does know we often prefer pico de gallo to regular salsa because it is crisp like a night in the desert.

I use the term *Hispano* because that is what Angie's family prefers. New Mexico is a unique state in many ways, one of which is the way many people identify themselves ethnically.

There are five major groups. In alphabetical order, they are Anglo, Chicano, Indian (or Native American), Hispano (or Spanish), and Mexican.

I'm not interested in the politics of labels. Or politics at all. So this is offered merely as fact. Most Indians I know refer to themselves by their tribe (e.g., Apache), or as Indians. Most of them do not use the term *Native American*. I rarely use either tribe names or the terms *Indian* or *Native American* because I call my friends by their given names.

Of course New Mexico also has a sprinkling of citizens whose ancestors came from Asia, Africa, Oceania, and almost everywhere else, but their numbers are statistically insignificant. As in they could all fit into the UNM basketball arena.

Hispanos are people whose ancestors came here more or less directly from Spain when what is now called New Mexico was part of New Spain. Many of them received land grants from the Spanish Crown. They do not identify with the country of Mexico or with the native peoples that were here before their arrival. A few people have seen them as racists because some Hispanos used the phrase *limpieza de sangre*, which means, roughly, "pure blooded." I have lived here for fifty years and never actually heard anyone use that phrase.

Some people I know have mailed off their saliva to 23andMe and reported that they are 100 percent Celtic or 100 percent Inuit or whatever, and so far as I know, no one considers such statements to be racist. The real question in my mind is why they care. I have no interest in having my genes identified because I know that even though my genes account for my physical features, they do not determine who I am. If I did believe that, I guess that would make me a determinist—someone who believes all things happen by cause and effect and therefore we have no control over them. I think that is not the same as predestination which applies only to your fate after you die. But I am a potter, not a philosopher, so don't take my word for it.

The terms *Mexican* and *Chicano* are seen by some people as synonyms. Others make this distinction: Chicanos are people whose families have been in New Mexico for a long time but did not come directly from Spain; i.e., they have a Mexican heritage.

Mexicans are people who have emigrated from Mexico more recently, roughly first- and second-generation newcomers.

Some people take these categories very seriously and are easily offended. Most people do not. I think the best route is not to put people in categories, but I admit I sometimes do. Like classifying Sharice as gorgeous.

The distinction between Hispanos and Chicanos and/or Mexicans is evident in curious ways. During Spanish Market events in Santa Fe, for example, you will see artisans selling traditional Spanish folk art such as *retablos*. But you will generally not see *serapes* and other products associated with Mexico. And you will not see a margarita stand (alas) because tequila is from Mexico, not Spain.

If you are wondering why I'm telling you about New Mexico's unique diversity, it's because the death of the man in the morgue can be fully understood only within that context.

I have created over the years a set of principles that I call Schuze Anthropological Premises, abbreviated SAP, which Susannah likes to jest is what you have to be to believe them.

SAP #1 is *Any human being can practice any culture*. You have to learn your culture; you are not born with it. It does not spring from your DNA.

According to the State Department, American families adopted about 81,600 babies from China between 1999 and 2018, the vast majority of whom were girls because of China's one-child policy. Those girls are ethnically Chinese, but they are now culturally Americans. They speak English as their first language. They prefer McDonald's French fries to tofu. Well, nobody said being American would make them healthier.

You know my first name is Hubie because that's what Tristan calls me, and now you know my last name is Schuze because that's how Angie addresses me.

I looked up *schuze* in the various dictionaries, directories, and encyclopedias in the library. The closest thing I found was *schůze*.

The *u* with the little circle over it is called *kroužkované u*. Looks like it could be the informal name of a university in a foreign country, but what it means is "overringed u," and it comes from the Czech language. The Czech word *schůze* means "meeting, session, or reunion."

Susannah's last name, Inchaustigui, is Basque. The closest I can come to telling you how to pronounce it is *In-chaus-teh-ghee*, accent on the second syllable, final syllable pronounced like the butter from India.

My thinking about the pronunciations of names likely resulted from the fact that it was May and the UNM graduation ceremony was scheduled for June. I'd served during the spring semester as interim head of the art department at UNM, and one of my upcoming duties was to attend the graduation and announce the names of the graduates from the art department as they walked across the stage to be handed their diplomas.

Susannah had seen me put my book away as she approached and asked me what I was reading.

"It's a book about Calvin."

"Ooh. I love Calvin."

"You do?"

Susannah is an intelligent woman with varied interests, but I was fairly certain theology was not one of them.

"You read Calvin?"

"Religiously," she said. "I like to quote him."

"You can quote Calvin?"

"Sure. Here's one. 'Your preparation for the real world is not in the answers you've learned, but in the questions you've learned how to ask yourself.'"

"Wow. I'm impressed." I figured she was quoting the more famous Calvin—John Calvin who led the reformation in the 16th century. I didn't want to dilute the joy of the moment by telling her I was reading about a different Calvin, one that few people outside of New Mexico have ever heard of. And not that many inside New Mexico for that matter.

She smiled that killer smile. "You think I'm just a simple cowgirl?"

"Not to insult cowgirls, but they don't normally have a graduate degree in art history."

"Which is why you hired me to teach art history."

"Right. And I hired you before I hired Freddie. And he has a doctorate and a lot more experience."

I hired both Susannah and Freddie as adjuncts for the spring semester. Adjuncts are part-time teachers who get paid by the course instead of being on a salary. They receive no health insurance or other benefits. I know all about being an adjunct because I served as one during the fall semester.

My experience that fall was memorable.

Traumatic might be a better word. A student in my class was murdered. The murderer turned out to be the department head, Milton Shorter. Shorter got the death penalty.

Not from the state; New Mexico abolished the death penalty in 2009. Shorter's death penalty was administered by his sister because he tried to frame her for the murder. She shot him through his office window. I was in the office at the time.

Whew!

The motto of the University of New Mexico is *Lux Hominum Vita*, which means "light the life of man." Probably needs updating because we no longer use *man* as a synonym for *human*.

But I have to say the shooting did in fact light my life—like staring into a klieg light at arm's length.

I became interim department head for the next semester because only one of the full-time faculty members wanted the job, and the rest of the faculty were unanimously against him getting it. I didn't seek the job. I got it by default.

Sort of the story of my life. I've never had a grand plan. Some of the kids I grew up with made lists of all the things they intended to do—what college they would go to, what they would major in, what sort of job they would take, where they would live, when they would get married, and how many kids they would have. I doubt that any of them thought about determinism or predestination, but if they believed in that sort of thing, there would be no reason to make a list. It had all been determined. All they had to do was wait and see.

They never included when they would die, but I secretly thought they might as well. Guessing when you'll die is no more difficult than guessing when you'll marry.

I didn't do much planning. I knew what college I'd go to because my father taught there, and it was three blocks from my house. I majored in pure math because I liked it, not because I had a plan. If I'd had a plan, I wouldn't have majored in pure math because there are no jobs it can lead to. People kept telling me that, so I finally got badgered into switching to accounting. And just as they had told me, it led to a job.

One that I hated. I stayed with the accounting firm for a couple of years before going back to UNM to study archaeology.

I can also quote Calvin (not Ross Calvin whom I was just now reading for the first time, but John Calvin the 16th century French theologian). He wrote, "God pardons our ignorance whenever something inadvertently escapes us."

As one who has had many things escape me, inadvertently or otherwise, I appreciate that quote. Now I was wondering to what extent, if any, my life had been determined by the New Mexico sky, the state's most dominant feature, infinitely large and impossibly blue.

I didn't complete the archaeology program, but I don't think it was because of the sky, which was the best part of being on digs. But that's another story.

The spring semester in the art department was much better than the fall one. Enrollment increased, grades were higher, we ended with a surplus rather than the deficit we had in the fall, Susannah and Freddie had terrific student evaluations, and no one was murdered.

All I had to do now was not mispronounce any graduate's name, and my semester as interim head would be a job well done.

Susannah said, "I know you hired me before you hired Freddie. But you didn't tell me you were hiring him. So I made a fool of myself when I ran into him between classes."

"Sorry. I thought you had forgiven me for that."

She sighed. "I have. Sorry to bring it up again. It's not your fault I haven't gotten over him."

I was happy to hear her say she hasn't gotten over Freddie. Susannah is the classic unlucky-in-love story. Which makes no sense. She's intelligent, good-looking, curvy, and fun to be with. And she's anxious to avoid the guilt she would feel about her mother's nervous breakdown if she isn't married before turning thirty.

Susannah once told me that when she was fourteen her

mother began telling her she hoped Susannah would meet a nice Basque young man to marry, preferably before Susannah reached her twenty-second birthday. When that didn't happen, Mrs. Inchaustigui widened the field from Basque young men to Catholic young men. As Susannah approached thirty, all unmarried Christian men were candidates, and for a while, Mrs. Inchaustigui, Mr. Inchaustigui, and their two sons seemed to believe I was the leading candidate. My gentle attempts to disabuse them of that notion always backfired, in part because Susannah refused to believe her family thought of us as a couple.

The family finally gave up when I moved in with Sharice, but they don't hold it against me, blaming their daughter for putting me off for so long.

Frederick Blass—Freddie—was the head of the art department before Milton Shorter. Freddie had to give up the job when he went to prison for manslaughter.

I know what you're thinking—one department head is sent to prison for manslaughter and his successor is murdered?

Look, it's just one of those quirks of history. Like John Wilkes Booth's brother saving Abraham Lincoln's son from death. Normally, UNM goes decades without anyone on the faculty being shot to death or imprisoned. Not that the university is likely to use that as the new motto when they get rid of the current politically incorrect one: *"The University of New Mexico—no faculty member shot to death or sent to prison for over a decade."*

Doesn't quite work for a recruitment brochure, does it?

Freddie got a light sentence which I suspect was because the jury was sympathetic to his claim of self-defense. He served his time, was a model prisoner, and received a commendation from the warden for teaching painting to his fellow prisoners which raised morale and decreased violence among the inmates.

I knew hiring an ex-con could be risky, so after Freddie's first week, I'd called Stella Ramsey, Channel 17's Roving Reporter, and asked her to do a story on Freddie's return to the university.

Stella is in great demand, but she made time to come to my

office because she and I had a brief fling a few years back. Actually she was the flinger, and I was the flingee.

She had seduced me those few years ago. Not that I put up much resistance. I doubt she was looking for a commitment. I was a lost puppy she could play with.

Her initial response as she walked into my office was "You want me to do a story on your magnanimous gesture?"

Stella is as blunt as she is beautiful, two attributes that make her a popular television news personality.

I told her I didn't want the story to be about me. I wanted her to interview Freddie's students.

"The ones hanging around in the hall," she asked.

"Yeah. I told them Stella Ramsey might be here. They probably want a selfie with you."

She smiled. "Bullshit. You made them hang around to encourage me to do a piece on Freddie."

I nodded. "Just talk to them."

She did, and the positive report she broadcasted pleased both Freddie and Dr. Gangji, the dean of the College of the Arts.

I took a sip of my margarita and suggested we change the subject.

"Okay," she said, "How about one of my pet peeves? Why do you always read weird stuff like a book about Calvin? You make fun of murder mysteries, but at least they have a plot, and often a lesson or inspiration. Does the book about Calvin have a plot?"

"It does not. So in that regard, it's just like real life."

"Lives have plots, Hubert."

I thought of my mother who called me Hubert only when she was annoyed.

Then I wondered why we call books about reality (biographies, histories, etc.) *nonfiction*, in effect defining them by what they are not. Wouldn't it be better to call books about real people and events *reality* and call made-up stories *nonreality*?

Then I answered Susannah's question. "Lives have *stories*, not plots. Some of them are fascinating. That's why I sometimes read biographies."

"A story and a plot are the same thing."

I shook my head. "I had a college friend named Henry Dennis Babers. Dennis, as he was called, went into the Marine Corps after we graduated. He died in the first Iraq war. His life is a story. He had family and friends, hopes and dreams, successes and failures. He served his country. In an unnecessary war in my opinion, but he felt honor-bound to serve. And he died at the age of twenty-three. His life did not have a plot. A life is a series of events and thoughts, but no author arranges them into a plot."

"God does that, Hubie. For every one of us."

I didn't want to argue with her on this issue because conversations about determinism and/or predestination make my head hurt. If God knows everything, then He knows what we will do. Which means we have to do it. For example, if He knows Susannah is going to order a second margarita, she has to order it. Not because God's spiritual hand takes hold of her physical one and forces her to wave to Angie, but because if Susannah *doesn't* order it, then God was wrong in *thinking* she was going to. And God can't be wrong.

Now my head is hurting just thinking about it. But I figured Ross Calvin would love it.

So I said, "You may be right. But I don't like to think God plotted a premature death into the story of Dennis Babers."

There was an awkward few seconds of silence before she said, "Let's have a second round."

She always orders a second round, but nevertheless a little chill ran down my spine.

After Angie had us reprovisioned, Susannah said, "What tidbits of wisdom are in that book?"

I hadn't found any from Ross Calvin because I was reading the biography first. So I gave her the John Calvin quote I've already mentioned. I said, "Here's one for you: 'God pardons our ignorance whenever something inadvertently escapes us.'"

She squinted. "Why is that quote for me? What has inadvertently escaped me?"

"The man who taught with you this spring is not the one who went to prison. He's the one who came out. He's a good man, Suze. And he's still in love with you. Always will be. I know you wanted nothing to do with him after he was convicted. But I've seen how you've softened. I see you chatting with him in the hall."

"You think I should get back together with him?"

"I think you should be open to the possibility. You know he sometimes joins Sharice and me for drinks when you aren't with us. Why don't you show up some evening and see what happens?"

She took a drink of her margarita and chewed the ice.

5

I was reading Ross Calvin when Stella Ramsey walked into my shop the next morning and announced she wanted to do a follow-up on her report on Freddie's hire.

"What kind of follow-up?"

"Don't be suspicious. Just because I like to dig for the truth doesn't mean I can't do feel-good stories. I suspect Freddie had a great semester. I'd like my public to know."

What I thought was, *my* public?

What I said was, "You don't need my permission to do a follow-up."

She smiled, and I remembered why I hadn't resisted.

"As a matter of fact," she said, "I do need your permission. Freddie said he wasn't doing anything public without your say-so."

"I guess as a former department head, he knows how difficult it is when a faculty member makes a public statement that reflects poorly on the department."

"I can't see him doing that," she said.

I smiled and said, "Neither can I. Unless your feminine wiles weaken him."

He and she had ended up in bed after the initial interview. I didn't know if Stella knew he told me, but she wouldn't care. She's a healthy woman with a strong libido and is able to separate sex from true affection. Good for her. Not the sort of person I'd want to have an ongoing relationship with, but that's a moot point. Stella doesn't do long term.

I remembered Freddie telling me that the three things he missed most in prison were freedom, sex, and booze. I guess after six years of celibacy, he was happy to lay eyes on Stella. On reflection, I could drop a couple of words from that sentence, but I think I'll just let it stand.

"You know all about my feminine wiles, Hubie."

"And remember all of them fondly."

"Of course you do."

The small pot Tristan had brought was still on the counter. Stella looked at it and said, "Doesn't look like one of those pre-Columbian ones you dig up."

"I know. I've never seen one like it, but I've come up with a theory about it."

When I hesitated, she asked, "Which is?"

"It may sound like a stretch, but I think it was used as a candle."

"How can you use a clay pot as a candle?"

"Simple. You fill it with buffalo fat, stick a wick in it, and light it."

"Yuk. I prefer one with lavender-scented wax. Wouldn't buffalo fat stink?"

"It wouldn't smell like lavender, but I don't think it would stink."

She asked why I thought earlier versions of the pot on my counter were used as candles.

"You know the Pueblo Indians have a long tradition of decorating the front of their homes with *farolitos* on Christmas Eve?"

"Everyone in New Mexico knows that."

"Right. They learned that custom from the Spaniards. *Farolito* means 'little lantern' in Spanish. A modern camping lantern has a light—usually lighted with butane—inside a glass. They didn't have butane or glass in New Mexico in the 17th century, so they—"

"I know," she said, "they used a candle inside a paper bag."

"No. We do that now, but the Pueblo Indians had no paper, and the Spaniards had very little paper. Only the leaders were literate, and they wouldn't have wasted what little paper they had on candles. But clay is everywhere. So I think the earliest *farolitos* were made of clay. This pot is new, but my guess is it's a copy of one from the 17th century."

She now had her notepad out, "So why would someone want a modern copy?"

I took a nicked-up clay jug from the shelf to my left and put it in front of her. "You've done reports on New Mexico's pottery. How would you describe this one?"

"Anasazi. And in fairly good shape considering its age."

I smiled. "Thanks for the compliment. This pot is less than two years old."

Now she was smiling. "One of your fakes. I should have guessed. So the answer to why anyone would want a modern copy of this strange little pot is they plan to sell it as genuine."

"That would be my guess."

In addition to not considering myself a thief, I also don't consider myself a swindler. My skills as a potter are good enough that I can make pots even an expert would identify as pre-Columbian. A few of them are in museums with labels to that effect, my name nowhere to be seen.

The ancients didn't sign their pots, and I follow their example. But I never lie about my copies. If a customer points to a pot I made and asks if it's genuine, I tell them it's a copy. Sometimes they will buy it anyway because they realize it will look just as good on the mantle as a real one would.

And it helps that I charge a lot less for a fake than a genuine Anasazi. But only if the buyer knows it's a fake. If someone walks in and buys a fake pot at the real pot price, that's his problem.

Except it's not really a problem is it? If he doesn't know it's a fake, he doesn't know he paid too much.

Stella frowned and said, "I still shudder when I hear the word *farolito*. In a stand-up last Christmas, I referred to the decorations here in Old Town as *luminarias*, and the station got a lot of calls complaining I used the wrong word. And some of the callers were really nasty. One even called me a *gringa* bitch."

"It's a sign of the times. People get bent out of shape over trivial things. Technically, *farolito* is a lantern and *luminaria* is a bonfire. Both are used at Christmas. But a lot of people have started calling the candles in paper sacks *luminarias,* especially in the southern part of the state and to a large extent here in Albuquerque. Almost everyone here in Old Town calls them *luminarias.*"

"So I wasn't wrong?"

I gave her my *luminaria* bonfire smile and said, "You're never wrong, Stella. And that comes from an expert."

She laughed and said, "Expert on me or on Spanish?"

She kissed me on the cheek, took a few pictures of the pot and headed to the door.

6

There were three reasons why I had to drive Sharice to her initial appointment with her obstetrician. The most important one was she wanted me to be with her. The other two were she doesn't have a car or a driver's license.

Her regular doctor, Linda Rao, had recommended someone named Dr. Chandra, but her practice was full, so Dr. Rao had arranged an appointment with Dr. Wójcik. As we rode to the office, Sharice Googled *Wójcik* and discovered there were two doctors with that in their name: Piotr Wójcik and Mei Zhen Chew-Wójcik.

She looked at me and said, "I suppose Dr. Rao mentioned the doctor's first name, but I don't remember which one it is."

"Definitely Mei Zhen."

"Glad you remembered."

"I didn't remember. Piotr is a male name. And I remember Dr. Rao referred to your obstetrician as *she*."

We were in the examination room for only a few minutes when the doc came in, glanced down at a clipboard, looked at Sharice and said, "Hi Sharice. I'm Mei Zhen Chew-Wójcik."

Then the doc looked at me and said, "And you must be the father."

"Yes," I said. And then remembering that I'm a decade older than Sharice who looks even younger than she is, I added "Of the baby, not of the Sharice."

32   J. MICHAEL ORENDUFF

She smiled and said, "You're not old enough to be her father. Or dark enough!"

We all laughed.

Then she said, "Glad you weren't offended. Because the UNM Medical College is unlike most other medical schools, we're sort of loosy-goosey here."

Sharice asked how the school was different.

Dr. Wójcik said, "Our official motto is 'Each of us defines all of us.' On our first day as new students, the dean of the first-year class said, 'We are the most diverse medical college in the country with a higher percentage of Hispanics and women than any other med school. So lesson number one is all of our spleens look alike!' He's a funny man, but we get what he means. We don't produce brain surgeons. Almost all of us are primary care doctors because that's what the small towns in New Mexico need. Nobody cares about skin color because we are all the same where it counts. I came here from China. One of the other foreign students was Piotr Wójcik from Poland. I fell for him despite his pale skin and weird eyes, and we married after we both graduated."

Sharice said, "I saw him on a list of MDs in Albuquerque, but the list didn't have specialties."

"He's a dermatologist. You and I don't have to worry much about the desert sun, but Hubie does." She turned to me and said, "You do wear sunscreen, right?"

"Uh . . ."

She reached into a pocket, pulled out a card, laughed, and handed it to me. "My husband's card."

Then she sat down next to Sharice. "Dr. Rao and I had a long consultation about you. I read all the records and examined all the scans. I have to be honest with you that I'm concerned, but only mildly so, about the tiny lump discovered in your right breast about two years ago. It hasn't moved or grown, and nothing in your lab results indicates that it's anything more than a milk gland filled with fluid. But I want you to keep track of it. I know it's almost too small to feel, but do self-exams frequently."

She paused for a moment then asked Sharice how she felt.

"Great" was her one-word reply.

THE POT THIEF WHO STUDIED CALVIN

"Glad to hear it. Some evidence suggests that the hormonal changes associated with pregnancy can increase the chances of a woman getting cancer, but that is true of all women, not just those who have had cancer. Most doctors recommend not getting pregnant sooner than two years after diagnosis. In your case it is well over five years. Now, lie down on the examination table and let me talk to your baby."

She poked and prodded and slid her stethoscope around. "You have . . . oops. I forgot to ask if you want to know how many and what sex."

"How many!" I said rather more loudly than I should have.

"We definitely need to know how many," said Sharice.

"One."

"Don't you need ultrasound to know that?"

"No. There is one heartbeat not counting your own. So what about the sex?"

"Hubie thinks he already knows it because of some wacky theory that couples who have sex more frequently are more likely to have a girl."

"Maybe not so wacky. The guy who did the research, Landrum Shettles, was a competent scientist. But there are also other factors that determine the likelihood of a girl or boy. Do you want to know which one you have?"

We looked at each other and said in unison, "No."

Dr. Wójcik asked me to wait in the lobby while she had a private moment with Sharice.

One the way home, I said, "I'm curious about the private chat you two had. But if it's confidential, I'll understand."

She laughed. "It's not confidential. In fact, it's two things you should know."

She smiled and hesitated.

"Well?" I finally said.

"First, she said it's healthy that we make love frequently."

"How does she . . . Oh, my comment about it being a girl."

"Right. And the second thing is you can do the breast exams. After all, you're the one who found the lump."

7

A few days later, a guy with a weird haircut and a weird accent came into my shop and asked, "¿Hablas español?"

I told him I did and then asked, "¿Hablas ingles?" and he told me he didn't.

I'll spare you having to translate.

He placed a pot on the counter.

I looked at it and blinked. It was identical to the one Tristan made.

"I am interested in a pot like this one," he said.

I reached under the counter, retrieved the one Tristan had given me, and placed it next to its twin. "Like this one?"

His eyes widened and he reached for it. I grabbed it and held it up for him to see, hoping he would think I did so in order for him to get a better look at it and not realize the real reason was I was afraid he'd grab it and run.

"How did you come to possess it?" he asked.

"The source of all my merchandise is confidential."

He stared at my pot for perhaps twenty seconds then looked up and said, "How much do you want for it?"

I could frame no immediate response because only questions came to mind; to wit, who was he, where did he get the pot he brought in, why did he want to know where I got mine, and why did he want to buy mine?

I thought of two possibilities, neither of which made sense.

Possibility one: He was Nomolos, the guy who commissioned Tristan to make the pots. But if that were the case, he already knew where the pot came from. And if he wanted another one, why not just make it? Tristan had already programmed his 3-D printer. All Nomolos would have to do is just fill the ink vat . . . er, clay vat, and turn the machine on.

Or maybe he offered to buy the pot not because he wanted it, but because he didn't want me to have it. He planned to mass produce clay *farolitos* and didn't want me as competition. If I didn't have one to copy, I wouldn't be able to make any.

Then I realized Nomolos spoke English to Tristan, so this guy wasn't Nomolos. Or maybe he was and for some reason didn't want me to know it. Maybe because he didn't want me to know he was the guy who hired Tristan. Why would he not want me to know that?

I added that question to the long list of other ones I had no answer for.

Possibility two: He bought the pot he had from Nomolos. But that also doesn't work. If he bought one from Nomolos, he could buy another one from him. It's not like the things were ancient one-of-a-kind specimens of the sort I dig up in the desert.

Sometimes I make snap decisions to do something weird just to see what happens. I looked him in the eyes and said, "I have this pot priced at five thousand dollars."

"Five thousand dollars! There is no way that pot is worth five thousand dollars."

"I'm in the pottery business, Mister . . ."

I waited for him to give me his name, but he just continued to stare at me as if I were crazy. And who could blame him?

So I continued. "The value of a pot is largely a matter of how rare it is. This is the only pot of this sort I've ever had in my shop. As you can see by looking around the shop, it is unlike anything else in my inventory. So its rarity is the reason for the price. Which is not high by comparison." I pointed to a genuine Anasazi pot similar to the fake I had shown Stella. "That pot is priced at fifty thousand, ten times more than this little rare one."

I hoped maybe throwing out a high price would induce him to tell me something about the pot and why he wanted it.

Which did not work.

"Your pot is not rare. You see another just like it right before your eyes."

"Mister . . . I don't think I caught your name."

"I didn't mention my name."

"Oh. Well, I know now that there are two of these pots. That is still few enough to qualify as rare."

"I'll give you a hundred dollars for it."

I returned the pot to its place under the counter.

"Two hundred," he said.

I shook my head.

"Five hundred."

I shook my head again. At this rate, it was going to take a while for him to reach $5,000.

But he stopped at $500, grabbed his pot, and walked out.

8

I put my copy of the 3-D pot in my secret hiding place. The guy seemed so intent on getting it, I feared he might try to steal it.

Then I drove to UNM because Dean Gangji had called a meeting of the department heads to prepare for the graduation.

"You will recall that in our last meeting of the semester, I was upset that enrollment in the theater department was down eleven percent. Music was down seven percent. Communications was down four percent. Dance was down eight percent."

He paused and gave us a stern look. With his full black beard and deep-set eyes, he does stern really well. "I did not mention enrollment in the art department because I didn't want to embarrass the four department heads who have served for years by pointing out that the new guy, Hubie Schuze, whose entire experience consists of teaching one course as an adjunct in the fall, managed to increase enrollment in his department by seventeen percent."

Despite his stern look, I sensed he was kidding us, and I said, "So instead of embarrassing them then, you embarrass me now because my term is over and you no longer have to deal with me."

Everyone laughed. Including the dean, who replied, "Your term is not over until after graduation. So do not provoke me."

More laughter.

Gangji said, "Our numbers may be down, but our quality is not. We have an excellent graduating class we can be proud of. We need to make sure this graduation goes well. And that we don't have another embarrassing incident like we did last year. Jim, please fill Hubie in on that."

Jim Shrader is the head of the music department, and he was an informal mentor for me when I was thrust into the interim art department head job.

"For many years," he began, "we lined the graduates up in alphabetical order. But it was always a struggle."

"They are artists," said the head of the theater department, laughing. "They don't know the alphabet."

"That may be true. But we do, and we are the ones who lined them up."

"But we couldn't keep them in line," the theater head added.

"True," said Jim. "After we had them in line, they would start to talk to a friend a few places behind or in front of them, or go to the restroom, or whatever. So when the process began, some big blond strapping lad would walk across the stage as the department head read out some name like 'Maria Martinez.' Some of the audience would laugh. The kid would stop, go over to the reader and whisper his name, then try again. It slowed down the already too-long event and made some parents angry that the department head didn't seem to know their son's or daughter's name."

"I have three hundred graduates," said the Communications Department head. "I can't be expected to know them all."

Shrader shot back, "Isn't that what the communications faculty teaches?" He smiled when he said it, but I sensed he was not entirely joking. "So, we gave up on alphabetical order and have the students line up as they please. The graduates write their name on a small piece of paper and hand it to the department head as they go across. So the name always matches the person approaching the dean who hands out the diplomas."

"But how can the dean hand out the right diplomas if he doesn't know who is next until the name is called?" I asked.

"He doesn't hand them a diploma. He hands them a diploma *cover*. It's bright red and has the seal of the university embossed in shiny silver. But it's empty. The actual diplomas are mailed out a few days later."

"Sounds foolproof," I said.

"Right. A fool can't mess it up. But a prankster can. Last year, a young woman who was not scheduled to graduate, who was not even enrolled, bought a cap and gown at the UNM bookstore. She showed up for the graduation, got in line, and wrote a name on a slip of paper. When it was her turn to walk across the stage, she handed the slip of paper to the department head who read the name she had written: *Jenna Tailia*."

I winced.

Jim looked at me and said, "Yeah. That's how we all felt. Half the people in the audience gasped, and the other half laughed. The young woman walked to the middle of the stage, faced the audience, lifted her gown to reveal her birthday suit, then ran down the aisle and out of the building. Turns out she was a stand-up comic in a local club, and her act drew full houses for weeks after the newspaper ran a story about her stunt."

The dean said, "We have four department heads with years of experience and one guy with virtually none who was expelled from the university. As a team, you should be able to come up with a plan to foil any prankster."

They all turned to look at me.

It was a summer dig to introduce the students to the harsh reality of being an archaeologist. I didn't fit in because I thought being out in the desert was fun, not harsh. What wasn't fun was using little brushes to clear away a millimeter of earth so as not to damage anything. As if we couldn't tell there was nothing there.

After enduring as much boredom as I could stand, I walked a couple of miles away from the official dig site to a place that looked like a location someone would actually seek. Including pre-Columbian people who may not have had writing, but knew how to read the land.

I dug up three beautiful pots. I felt the warm hand of the woman who made them. I'm a born mathematician, not a psychic or new-ager. I know a thermometer would have shown the pots had the same temperature as the sand they had been rescued from. Feeling her hands was not physical; it was mental. Which for a math guy is more real than the senses.

I thought the head of the archaeology program who was leading the dig would be happy I'd made a find. But he scolded me for digging away from the site and demanded that I turn the pots over to him.

It was before the passage of the Archaeology Resources Protection Act, so I had the legal right to keep the pots.

But I also understood why he was upset. Archaeologists dig to gain knowledge of past cultures. The knowledge gained is only valid if there is site integrity. A pot taken out of the ground and clandestinely spirited away leaves behind the context of the find.

But it was clear from his anger that Gerstner, the leader, was upset mainly because he thought I had made him look bad for selecting a barren piece of land to excavate. I read the terrain better than he did and intuitively knew where the ancient ones would have built.

And I had carefully examined the site I dug in and was trying to tell him about it when he exploded in front of the other students.

I consulted the woman who made the pots I found. She told me to take the pots and run; she wanted them admired, not hidden in a basement lab.

And that's why I was expelled. Just another example of a life not planned.

I made sure the pots found good homes with people who understood and appreciated them.

And had enough money to buy them. I used the money for two down payments, one for the east third of the building in Old Town, and the other for a Ford Bronco, whose four-wheel drive has taken me across the deserts and up into the mountains in pursuit of ancient pots.

But now my life seemed to be changing. It was almost a year since I'd illegally unearthed a pot. I had a respectable job as department head, even if it was temporary. I was going to get married and have a child. In short, I was becoming Mr. Average Citizen.

I didn't plan it. Did God plan it as Susannah suggested? I didn't think so. I figured God had better things to do than wonder whether I got a real job. I love the New Mexico sky, but I hadn't yet been convinced that it explains as much as Ross Calvin claimed.

But I did like the way things were going. And didn't want to mess things up by trying to plan everything in advance. I was, as they say these days, going with the flow.

9

I returned from the graduation planning meeting just in time to walk to Dos Hermanas where I found Susannah, Tristan and Martin Seepu waiting for me, already with a margarita, a Corona, and a Dos Equis respectively.

Tristan also had his book bag with him which he normally does not drag along to the cocktail hour.

I met Martin Seepu when I volunteered for a program run by the University of New Mexico Indigenous Peoples Center that gave UNM students a chance for public service on the reservations. I was supposed to tutor kids who had dropped out of school and encourage them to go back to class.

Martin was a fourteen-year-old grade school drop-out. At our first meeting, he told me he had no intention of going back to school. He liked to learn. He just didn't like to do it in a classroom. So I taught him math because that's what I was majoring in at the time. In no time at all, he was able to do undergraduate math. He listened and he learned. And unlike college students who are required against their will to take algebra as a general education course, Martin never asked, "What good is this?" or "How is knowing this going to help me?"

Martin raises horses and I throw pots, so math is of no practical use to either one of us, but I think it shaped the way we think and gave us a bond. Martin was a taciturn kid. Explaining proofs to me helped him be at ease verbally, something not expected of children in his culture.

I told the gang about the customer with the strange haircut who spoke to me in strangely-accented Spanish, and who wanted to know where I got the 3-D printed pot and also wanted to buy it.

"Who did he turn out to be?" Susannah asked.

"No one."

"He turned out to be no one?"

"Well, he must be someone. But he wouldn't give me his name."

"So you have no idea who he might be?"

"At first I thought he might be Nomolos. But then I remembered Nomolos speaks English."

"Who is Nomolos?" she asked.

Tristan said, "He's the guy who paid me to make the pots." Then he filled them in about the 3-D printing job he had done.

I asked Tristan if Nomolos had a weird haircut.

"I don't know. He had some other guy deliver all the stuff I needed. I talked to Nomolos only by phone."

"Did he *sound* like someone with a weird haircut?"

After they stopped laughing, Susannah asked me to describe the haircut.

"It was like mine on the sides, normal length and combed down. But the hair on the top of his head was like a separate little patch. It was black like the rest of his hair, but it was shaped like a turned-over shallow bowl."

Martin said, "Maybe he had a bowl haircut. Some people on the rez do it because it's easy."

Susannah said, "The bowl used for a haircut usually covers the whole head, not just the top part. I know exactly what it was in this case. He's going bald on top like you, Hubie, and the separate patch up there was hair transplants."

"I'm not bald," I protested.

"Not yet, anyway. But you're headed in that direction."

Another laugh at my expense.

Susannah got Angie to bring a pocketbook mirror. She put her own mirror above the back of my head where it reflected onto Angie's mirror in front of me.

There was a thinning area back there. I had no idea. I mean, who looks at the back of their head?

"Just a little thinning," I said. "Nothing to worry about."

"That's what Dwayne 'The Rock' Johnson said," Susannah quipped.

Tristan's explanation that this Johnson fellow is a popular, strong, and handsome African American actor didn't help much. Black guys look good bald. Big guys look good bald.

Short white guys not so much.

Susannah asked what kind of a name Nomolos is, and I said it was Hispanic.

"I've never heard of it," she said.

"Neither have I."

"Then how do you know it is Hispanic?"

"Because he looked Hispanic."

She grinned and said, "You're not supposed to say someone looks Hispanic, Hubie."

I sighed. "Okay. He had black hair, light tan skin, and speaks only Spanish."

"How do you know he speaks only Spanish?"

She loves trying to throw me off stride.

"I don't know it, but I think it's likely. He told me he doesn't speak English. It's possible he speaks Urdu or Swahili, but for most people who speak a second language, that second language is English. So I assume he's not bilingual. And on top of that, *Nomolos* has the alternate consonant-vowel pattern of most Spanish names like Morales, Romero, Molina, Ramírez, and hundreds more."

"But how come none of us have ever heard of the name Nomolos?" Tristan asked.

"There are hundreds, maybe thousands of Hispanic names we've never heard of. And I told you he had a strange accent. He's probably from someplace like Chile, or Spain, or Catalonia."

"I thought Catalonia was part of Spain."

"The Spanish also think that, but a lot of Catalonians don't. And Catalonian doesn't sound exactly like Spanish."

"So he may have been Catalonian?"

I shook my head. "Seems like a long shot. I just threw that in as an example. How many Catalonian tourists visit Old Town, and what are the odds one would have a pot with him and know I had one just like it?"

Susannah said, "He must be a local."

"Yeah," I said. "But why the strange accent?"

She plopped her margarita down on the table and scanned us. "Because it's part of his ploy!"

Here we go again, I thought.

"What ploy?" Martin asked.

"I don't know. Yet. But here's what we *do* know. He wants Hubie's pot, and he also wants to know where it came from. Which means he wants to get other ones. These pots are important to him in some way. So he has a ploy. And it requires him to operate incognito. So he faked an accent."

I thought about it for a few seconds before saying I didn't think he could fake an accent.

"Actors do it every day, Hubie."

"Yeah. But they have lines and can practice. This guy—"

"Let's give him a name!" Susannah interrupted with enthusiasm.

"Why?" Tristan asked.

"Because it's easier and more fun than calling him 'the guy who walked into Hubie's store and faked an accent.'"

"He didn't fake an accent," I insisted.

"You can explain that after we name him."

"Fine," I said as I threw up my hands. "How about Arcilla?"

"I like it!" she said. "So why can't Arcilla fake an accent?"

"Because he can't predict what I might ask him, so he can't practice in advance like an actor. And when he responded to what I said, he did so quickly and naturally. Furthermore, his accent was consistent. Weird, but consistent. No way could someone do that."

She looked a little disappointed.

Then she brightened. "He came into your shop!"

Martin, Tristan, and I looked at each other then at her.

"Come on guys. You can figure out what that means."

We continued to stare at her until Tristan said, sort of triumphantly, "There's a picture of him. Two actually. One coming in, and one coming out."

"What are we waiting for?" asked Susannah, "Let's go."

10

I have only two margarita glasses at my shop, so I asked Angie if Susannah and I could borrow the two we had just used. She agreed since they were empty, and we wouldn't be violating the open container law.

Not that it mattered. It's not enforced in Old Town unless you appear to be under the influence. Deeply under.

After I unlocked the shop, I brought my laptop up from under the counter, and we gathered around it.

Usually, I have Tristan do anything that needs doing on the little laptop he gave me, but he was hauling his book bag back to my living area, so I opened the file where the pictures are, and we saw ourselves coming into the shop. We looked like late night revelers.

The camera is tiny and sits on the top shelf. It takes a picture of the door every time it opens. Tristan installed it as an upgrade to my previous system which was a bell attached to the door.

I pushed a key on the laptop, and a different picture appeared showing a man exiting the shop.

"There he is," said Susannah. "He looks shifty, like someone with a ploy."

I said, "That's a guy who came in to ask for directions to Dos Hermanas. He was sitting at the table next to us."

The next picture—they are obviously arranged in reverse chronological order—was the same guy coming into the shop.

"Right," said Susannah, "that *is* the guy from the next table. I'd recognize him anywhere."

I said nothing.

Martin said, "I only got a glance at him because his table was behind Tristan who blocked my view."

When Tristan returned, we were looking at the picture of Arcilla as he departed.

Tristan said, "I see what you mean about the haircut. Does look like you, Uncle Hubie."

"It does not look like me. I don't have that sort of ring shape around the middle patch."

The accent turned out to be the third clue. In retrospect, I probably would have realized that the hair was a fourth clue, but I was too focused on defending my non-baldness to see the hair issue from a perspective other than via two make-up mirrors.

"Forget the hair," I said, "let's get back to the accent. Where do people speak Spanish that doesn't sound like what we hear every day in New Mexico?"

Susannah said a geologist she knows named Thom told her that in some of the northern New Mexico villages, people still speak an archaic 17th-century version of Castilian. Thom used to go there on business and be peered at from behind blinds and be talked in front of in the odd dialect.

"That might explain it," I said.

Martin said, "Or he could be from a reservation."

We stared at him.

"The Spaniards made us speak their language, but of course we didn't speak it like the learned people in the court of King Philip II. Then the Americans stole New Mexico from Mexico and made us all speak English, so our Spanish got even worse because we had to concentrate on a new language."

"That could also explain it," I said.

He smiled and continued. "Been good for us to be bilingual. We can travel from the northernmost tip of Canada speaking

English and switch to Spanish as we go south all the way to the tip of Tierra del Fuego."

I changed the subject by asking Tristan if Nomolos could make more pots easily now that the 3-D printer was programmed.

"As long as he wants them to look like the ones he already has, it's a piece of cake."

"So why would the guy who came to my shop want to buy mine if he can get all he wants from Nomolos?"

"Maybe he was looking for a bargain," said Martin. "You deal only in Indian pots, so maybe he figured you'd let this modern thing go cheap."

"He may not have known it was modern."

"What did he offer for it?"

"A hundred dollars."

"Then he must have known it was modern. Old ones can run well into the thousands."

Tristan said, "A hundred dollars is a good price for it. It probably cost only about four dollars to make. If people are willing to pay a hundred dollars for those, you should buy me a 3-D printer, Uncle Hubie. We could make a fortune. You sold it to him, right?"

"No."

"Why not? You already knew how cheap and easy it was to make."

"I told him I had it priced higher than that."

He squinted at me. "How much higher?"

"Five thousand dollars."

"Five thousand dollars!" they shouted in unison, sounding like a trio with Susannah in her mezzo-soprano, Martin in his baritone, and Tristan in his bass.

Susannah added, "What were you thinking?"

"I was thinking something fishy was going on. Who was he? Where did he get the pot? Why did he want another one? How did he know I had one? So I figured I'd throw out a ridiculous price to rattle him. And I thought he might make a counteroffer. Which he did. He offered me the hundred. When I turned that down, he offered me two hundred and then five hundred, which I also turned down."

Tristan was amazed. "Why would you turn down five hundred dollars for a four-dollar pot?"

"Because if I sell it, I'll never know the answer to all those questions I just asked."

"What if he had agreed to the five thou?" asked Susannah. "Would you have taken it?"

"Absolutely."

"Then you would also never have known the answers."

"True. But I'd have been well-paid for my ignorance."

11

How about a nightcap?" I asked.

We'd had only one round at Dos Hermanas, but the main reason I wanted to fix a second one was to show off the birthday present Tristan had given me.

For the first forty-nine years of my life, my birthday was celebrated on May 5th. I liked that it was *Cinco de Mayo*. Then I discovered I was actually born on May 1st. May Day is not nearly so cool as *Cinco de Mayo*, but May 1st is on my birth certificate that I saw for the first time a little over a month ago.

I'll spare you the story. Unless it somehow ties in.

Tristan's gift was a *Margaritaville Frozen Beverage Maker*. There was a picture of Jimmy Buffett on the box.

The machine stands a foot-and-a-half high, weighs in at sixteen pounds, and has a 400-watt motor that shaves ice and blends the liquids simultaneously into a built-in pitcher.

For those who are measurement challenged (Quick—How many ounces in a half gallon?), it comes with a no-brainer carafe that has markings up the side. Tequila to the first line, triple sec to the second line, lime juice to the third line, etc. Then pour it into the machine and hit start.

It sounds like an outboard motor, but after a while, the noise is part of the fun.

I've found the carafe less reliable on subsequent batches because I'm more likely to confuse *triple sec to the second line* with *double sec to the triple line*.

The margarita machine was the hit of the impromptu party.

Tristan was pleased that I raved about his gift, and Martin was so infatuated with the device that he switched from beer to a margarita.

We were having a great time until Freddie walked in. He was able to do so because he has the key I gave him when I picked him up on the day he was paroled and took him to my shop where he's been living in the back because he had no other place to go. Of course I was already living in Sharice's condo, so the back of the shop was vacant.

When Mr. Clarke showed up, I had to move back to the living quarters behind Spirits in Clay.

I bought the middle unit of the building a few years back and ran a second shop in it, but it was more hassle than it was worth, so I now rent it to Gladwyn Farthing who runs a shop with the cringe-worthy name F°ahrenheit F°ashions where he sells casual clothing that he describes as jumpers, plimsolls, and swimming costumes. If he were from the US instead of the UK, he'd call them sweaters, athletic shoes, and swimsuits. But he's not and he doesn't, and I don't try to change him because I like his accent.

My move back to Spirits in Clay forced Freddie into moving temporarily next door to F°ahrenheit F°ashions. There's no living quarter, but there is a bathroom, and he's sleeping on a bedroll. I've asked him to keep an eye on my property, so of course the loud noise from the machine woke him, and he came in to see what was going on.

And a heavy blanket of unease flopped over us.

Everyone in the room knew Freddie and Susannah's history. Everyone knew not to mention it when we were gathered at Dos Hermanas.

So we just stood there, our tongues on display because our jaws had dropped.

Until I walked over to The Machine and turned it on.

The roar gave everyone a start, and Freddie said, "What the hell is that thing?"

"A margarita machine," I said.

Susannah, although she can stick a glowing red branding iron on a two-thousand-pound bull without flinching, is not known for aplomb in social settings. But she took in a deep breath, smiled, and said to Freddie, "Can I get you a margarita, cowboy?"

12

Susannah and Freddie were the first to leave.

They weren't hand in hand or anything, but that didn't stop Martin from saying, "They were looking at each other like they did back when they were dating."

"That's a good sign," I said.

"Not if it ends like their first courtship."

"I'm not worried about that. They may not get back together, but if they do, I don't think anyone is going to be killed or go to prison."

I wish I hadn't said it.

After Martin left, Tristan looked at me apprehensively and asked if he could spend the night in the shop with me.

"Sure. But what's the problem?"

"I didn't want the others to hear about it. Someone broke into my apartment this afternoon and ransacked the place."

If the topic had been lighter, I would have asked him how he knew his apartment had been ransacked; it always looks that way. Instead I asked if he'd called the police.

"Yeah. They came, looked around the place, and said it looked like it had been ransacked."

"Good to have a professional assessment of what you already knew."

"They took some prints but warned me that they are most likely mine or from a friend. They had me make a list of everyone who'd been in the apartment in the last few months."

"You remembered them all?"

"I may have missed one or two. There was you, my mom, some guys I hang out with, and some girls."

"Are you worried that some of the girls may not appreciate that being in your apartment led to them being fingerprinted?"

"I feel bad about it. But there are about fifteen thousand girls at UNM, so having a dozen or so mad at me isn't a major issue."

"I suppose they had you make a list of things that were missing?"

"Right. But nothing was missing."

"Nothing!"

"Nothing."

It came to me immediately. "They were looking for pots."

He frowned. "Pots?"

"Yeah. Remember we were talking about the guy with the weird accent and haircut and how intent he was on getting my pot? Well, he must have been intent on getting yours as well."

"I don't have any."

"I know that. But he doesn't. And he must have known you were the one who made the copies for Nomolos."

"How would he know that? I didn't tell anyone but you."

"But Nomolos knew, and the guy he sent to deliver the stuff to you knew, and who knows who else he may have told? His wife? A neighbor? As Winston Churchill said, 'two people can keep a secret if one of them is dead.'"

He thought for a moment. "I think you're right. It had to be Nomolos. He saw the picture of the pot in the *Albuquerque Journal* and realized I made an extra copy. Which made him wonder how many extras I'd made. So he broke in to find out."

"What picture in the paper?"

He laughed. "I forgot you don't read the paper or watch TV. Stella Ramsey reported on your unusual pot in her evening spot on the TV news, and the *Journal* must have thought it was an interesting story because they did a follow-up piece."

* * *

Suddenly it all made sense. Nomolos had two friends, or employees, or whatever—the one who delivered the stuff to Tristan, and the one who came to my shop. They couldn't be the same person because Tristan saw them both. Of course Nomolos could have been the guy who came to my shop. But whether it was Nomolos and one sidekick or Nomolos and two sidekicks, he and/or a sidekick or two had broken into Tristan's apartment after they saw the picture of the pot in the paper or on TV. I felt a little less foolish about hiding the copy Tristan had made for me. And lucky because no one had broken into my shop.

But not terribly surprised. Old Town is patrolled. My place is alarmed. Between Freddie and Gladwyn, there is usually someone there. It's much easier to skulk around in Tristan's student ghetto than to do so in Old Town.

And there was one more reason why they hadn't broken into my place. Yet. They knew I had a pot. And they were probably confident that I had only the one, given to me by my nephew.

What they didn't know was how many other copies Tristan may have made without their knowledge.

After all, when Nomolos got the partial bag of clay back, how would he know if the portion of it Tristan used was just the right amount to make the eight pots Nomolos had asked for? I'm a potter, but I can't tell you exactly how much clay any particular size and shape of pot will take. It doesn't matter in my case because I'm sitting at a wheel with clay and water by my side. If I need a bit more clay, I just scoop it up and mold it into my project. Usually, I err in the other direction and have clay left over when the pot begins to take shape, so I dump the extra back into the clay bag.

So I figured they hit Tristan's apartment because it might contain any number of copies. Not just a few extras from the clay they delivered to Tristan, but he could have bought more clay for all they knew and made a hundred of the things.

I was buoyed by the pleasurable feeling of having reasoned out what had happened.

Which evaporated when I realized I had no idea *why* it had happened. Why would they care if Tristan made an extra and gave it to his uncle who was in the business? If they wanted only eight, why would they care if I had one? Or if Tristan had a few?

Jealousy? Doesn't seem like something worth committing burglary for, but people sometimes blow things way out of proportion. I wouldn't want someone to copy a pot I designed, but I wouldn't break in to steal it. And they didn't design the pot; it was centuries old. All they did was copy it. And they could make as many copies as they wanted to.

13

I was surprised when Whit Fletcher showed up early the next morning.

Not about the early part; he's irritatingly consistent. It was the showing up part that surprised me. He's not prescient, so he wasn't looking into the murder that hadn't yet happened. Of course I didn't think about that because I didn't know about it either.

"You don't look too happy to see me, Hubie."

"You're a trained detective, Whit. Notice I'm wearing boxer shorts and a tee-shirt? And that my hair is uncombed and there's sleepy seeds in my eyes? I was in bed."

"Then you should thank me for waking you up so's you don't waste the whole day. How about you make some coffee?"

He followed me back to the living space and looked out into the courtyard.

"You know someone's sleeping in your hammock?"

"Yeah. It's Tristan."

"What I figured. Probably don't want to stay in his place that was burgled."

"How'd you know that?"

"Like you said, I'm a trained detective."

"And head of the homicide division, so why are you working a burglary case?"

"I'm not. But the chief usually mentions some of the new cases at the morning briefing, and this morning he mentioned a bunch of break-ins. When there's more of any sort of crime than average, the chief gets worried because he knows the public will get worried. And there's been a lot of break-ins recently."

"So you want to talk to Tristan about it?"

"I do. But not officially."

"How'd you know he'd be here?"

He smiled. "Actually, I wanted to talk to you. I figured Tristan would be asleep. Only I didn't figure he'd be doing it in your hammock. Handy for me I can talk to both of you."

"You didn't think I'd be asleep?"

"I knew you would. But Tristan is a kid, parties hard and late. You're a grown man; you need to get up and do something."

I'd hit the brew button on the coffeemaker while Whit was talking. I poured two cups and sat down.

He sat down and took a sip. "What got me thinking was that all the break-ins the chief mentioned were in a neighborhood where people own stuff worth stealing. Tristan's place was the only one in a low-rent area. Maybe there's a burglar out there too stupid to know the poor got nothing to steal. And I'd normally put Tristan in that 'nothing to steal' category. But he has an uncle who deals in pricey merchandise. What can you tell me, Hubie?"

"You may be on the right track."

His eyes didn't light up. I've never actually seen anyone's eyes light up. I don't think it's possible. What happens is someone gets good news and they smile, which stretches their face and makes their eyes more noticeable because there is less skin bunched up around them, and therefore more light is reflected from them. There are no phosphorescent cells in the eyes. I explained this theory to Susannah once and she called me a "good-news Scrooge," so I haven't mentioned it since.

But regardless of what his eyes showed, everything else about him was happy.

Whit is a good cop. He hunts down criminals relentlessly. He's gotten a lot of dangerous people off the streets. He's earned a bunch of honors.

If there is a blemish in his career, it's that he occasionally comes into money as a result of a case he worked on. I hasten to add he'd never take a bribe. They haven't printed enough money to make him overlook a misdemeanor, much less a felony. But if he's searching a thief's den and finds a wad of cash that isn't needed to prosecute said thief because there are tons of stolen goods as evidence, then most or all of the cash winds up in Whit's pocket. I assume not for long. He probably has an even better hiding place than I do.

And he wouldn't want to embarrass his mother if he were in a serious auto accident and it was revealed that he had unaccounted-for cash in his pocket and was wearing dirty underwear.

I told him about the pots Tristan had made and how I thought that was what the thief was looking for.

I went to the front, got my laptop from under the counter, took it back to my kitchen table and showed Whit the pot Arcilla had brought. You could see it in the picture of Arcilla coming in because he had it in his hand.

"Thing's tiny," Whit observed. "Something sorta plain and small like that can't be worth much."

"Could be worth a fortune if's genuine. But it's a modern copy."

"You've made a pretty good living selling fakes to folks who think they're real."

"That's because my fakes look like they're old. This little one wouldn't fool anyone, it's too perfect."

He pointed to the fake Anasazi I'd shown Stella. "I know you made that one. And you put a bunch of cracks in it and a hole you can stick your fist through. Why not do something similar to the one little one you've got to make it look old?"

"Because it's the *inside* that shows it's new. It was copied from an old one, so the outside looks exactly like an old one. But the inside is too perfect because the copying was done by a 3-D printer. A 3-D printer is—"

"I know what a 3-D printer is. We've got four of 'em at the station. And we didn't even have to use taxpayer money for one of 'em. We confiscated it from a guy who was using it to make gun parts."

Scary. I could understand how a crook could use one. But

what would the police do with one? I pictured Whit duplicating a pair of handcuffs with a 3-D printer. "Why would cops want 3-D printers?"

"Lots of law enforcement agencies use 3-D printers for things like making crime scene models to help them present cases in court. We've always used models, but the 3-D printers do it faster and better. They can also reproduce fingerprints, tire tracks, and other sorts of evidence. And they also have a more gory use."

"I don't need to know that."

But he plowed ahead. "The badly decomposed remains of a murdered woman were found in the woods near Dayton, Ohio a few years back. Because of the condition of the body, all attempts to identify the victim failed. So the police used 3-D printing to make a copy of the victim's skull. They then added plastic skin, ears, a nose, etc. After images of the model were released to the public, a few people recognized her and reported it to the police. Knowing who had been killed enabled the police to find and arrest the murderer."

I wondered briefly if a 3-D copy of Arcilla's hair shape could be used to discover his identity.

"Let's get back to the pots," I said. "The problem here is the inside is perfect. If I try to make this one look old and it doesn't work, I won't have a second chance because I have only one pot."

"Just have Tristan make some more."

"He no longer has access to the 3-D printer he used."

Whit smiled, and I thought I might have to rethink my eyes-lighting-up theory.

"I know where I can lay my hands on one," he said.

14

Whit finally gave up on Tristan waking up and left around eleven.

Waking Tristan is actually easy if you have a train whistle or chorizo.

I sliced the skins off a few of the plump little sausages and squeezed their contents into a frying pan. No need for olive oil or lard; chorizo has its own supply of orange grease. I added sliced jalapeños and diced tomatoes, and gave it a stir. I placed six blue-corn tortillas on my *plancha*, and chopped up some cilantro. When the tortillas had a few grill marks, I flipped them so both sides would be crunchy. Then I dabbed the chorizo mixture on them, added some Hatch green chile, tossed the cilantro on them, and folded them over.

Tristan shuffled to the bathroom while I was finishing up and came out just in time for breakfast tacos. He ate four and drank coffee. I ate the other two and had a few sips of Gruet Blanc de Noir. I limited myself to the sips because it was less than six hours to margaritas.

New Mexico's greatest contributions to the world—in alphabetical order—are Gruet Champagne, Hatch green chile, the Roswell Aliens, Rudolfo Anaya, and Tony Hillerman.

After Tristan inhaled the tacos, he asked me if I thought it was safe for him to return to his apartment.

"Should be. The people looking for the pots now know there aren't any there, so they have no reason to come back."

"What if we're wrong about that, and it was just a regular burglary?"

"In that case, they already know there's nothing they want because they looked everywhere but took nothing."

"But maybe they started thinking about it and decided there are a few things they could use?"

I started to shoot that one down as well until it clicked—he didn't want to go back yet.

So I said, "Here's what we know for certain: nothing."

He laughed and relaxed.

"The wisest move," I said, "is for you to stay here a few days. Maybe the cops will make some progress. And I'd like the company."

"Great. I have a temporary job today at the registrar's office, but I'll be back in time for dinner."

I asked him what kind of work was going to do at the registrar's office.

"They want me to make sure their records are up-to-date regarding graduation."

"Isn't that part of their job?"

"It is. And so is a lot of other stuff. The problem is the departments and colleges are always tampering with their graduation requirements. For example, my department, computer science, has always required algebra. Last year, they decided to give students a choice between algebra and symbolic logic. But it took the change a while to get approval from the dean, then the academic vice president, and then the faculty senate. A few of my fellow computer science majors went ahead and took symbolic logic instead of algebra. But they didn't show up on the list of graduates because the change hadn't been entered into the Banner Software. It was all worked out after the fact, but caused a lot of anxiety. Because the time leading up to graduation is the second busiest for the registrar after registration itself, they don't have time for last minute checks. So they hired me to look at every approved change, check to see if it's in the software, and add it if it isn't."

When I became interim head with only a few days' notice, Tristan was my unofficial assistant department head because he knew how to use the software. If you are like I was, you probably believe the university is run by faculty and staff. In fact, it is run by the software.

After Tristan left, I began to feel guilty about his being involved in the pot thing. From a purely rational point of view, I had not involved him. He had taken on the 3-D printing job on his own and made an extra one for me on his own.

But the purely rational point of view felt more like rationalization than reason. Maybe part of his decision to take on the pottery copying job was that I was in the business. A business that started when I was expelled. A business based in large part upon digging up ancient pots, an activity that became illegal when the Federal Government passed the Archaeological Resources Protection Act. A business that had led Arcilla to my shop and maybe burglars to Tristan's apartment.

My only valuable possessions are the building in Old Town and my inventory of pots. But neither of those count as possessions in my view. My name is on the title of the east two-thirds of the building, but the structure has been there since 1680 and will be there long after I am gone. It is not transitory; I am.

The pots do not belong to me just as the *Mona Lisa* does not belong to the Louvre even though that's where it's housed. The *Mona Lisa* belongs to Leonardo da Vinci and always will. The pots belong to the women who made them and always will. I am their caretaker, not their owner.

15

Susannah asked me how the visit to the obstetrician went.

"It was good. In fact it was fun. Dr Wójcik seems extremely competent and has a great sense of humor."

"What sort of name is Wójcik?"

"Polish. But that's because she's married to a Polish guy. Her first name is Mei Zhen; she's ethnic Chinese."

"Excellent! Sharice now has an Indian cancer doctor and a Chinese obstetrician."

"Why is that excellent?"

"Because Indians and Chinese make the best doctors. Everyone knows that, Hubie. My mother always told me, 'Make sure your doctor is Indian or Chinese.'"

"What about a Basque doctor?"

"Never heard of one. I suppose there are some in Spain, but I don't think there are any here. My mother would have known about that and tried to fix me up with him."

I knew I should drop the topic, but I couldn't resist asking why Indians and Chinese made the best doctors.

"Because they're generally smarter than other people."

"There is a lot of scientific evidence that shows no ethnic group is innately smarter than any other," I said

"I know that. It's not that they are *innately* smarter. It's just that they become smarter because when they are in the most crucial years for brain development, their brains are stimulated more than kids from other cultures."

"Why is that?"

"Because while all other kids in the world are learning the alphabet which is twenty-six letters for most of them, the Chinese kids are learning over fifty thousand characters."

"And the Indian kids?" I couldn't resist asking.

"Because while all other kids in the world are learning about God, Jesus, Mohammed, and maybe a few disciples, Indians are learning fifty Hindu Gods, each one of whom has about fifty incarnations for a total of 2,500, and there's a story attached to each one. Makes sense, right? As Calvin said, 'New ideas are thrust at you every day.' So now you know why Indian and Chinese doctors are the best."

"So what have you been up to?" I asked to change the subject and to avoid telling her that the Calvin I was reading was not the Calvin she was quoting.

"I've been thinking about the mystery of your little pot. I think the guy's accent is a clue. A good title would be *The Clay Candleholder Caper*."

"It might be a bit premature to give it a title, much less make it a murder mystery. It's confusing, but nothing is riding on it."

She tilted her head forward and whispered, "Tell the truth. After the mysterious stranger left, you put that little clay pot in your hidey-hole didn't you?"

"I did, but—"

"Because you were afraid he might try to boost it."

"Boost it?"

"You know, shoplift, grab, pinch, filch."

"He did seem determined. And he wouldn't give me his name. I suppose I didn't really think he would break in, but you can't be too careful."

"Right. You've got half a million in irreplaceable ancient inventory sitting on open shelves, but you put a four-dollar 3-D printed pot in a place no one can get to."

"I'm not worried about my inventory. Thanks to Tristan, I have security cameras and alarms, and we have night patrols in Old Town."

"Then why hide the pot?"

"Maybe it doesn't make much sense in retrospect, but I had the feeling he was determined to get that pot. No one's after the stuff on the shelves, so the imminent threat gets more attention than a theoretical one."

"Weak," she said.

I lofted my margarita. "I'll drink to that."

She laughed and took a sip. "I've decided you're right about the accent. He couldn't have faked it."

"What made you change your mind?"

She took a sip of her margarita, thought for a moment and asked me if I knew about the so-called war of accents in the 1930s in Hollywood.

I admitted I did not.

Susannah loves old films. When she was a young girl, she idolized Merle Oberon, and she can quote long passages of dialog from *The Scarlet Pimpernel* and *Wuthering Heights.*

"Well," she began, "America had a virtual world-wide monopoly on the production and distribution of films back in the '30s. American films were shown almost everywhere. The studio bosses realized that the second most widely spoken language in our hemisphere is Spanish. So they started making Spanish-language versions of their films. When the Spanish-language films first hit theaters in Latin America, ticket sales were great. But that changed quickly. The actors in the films were from Spain, Mexico, Columbia, Argentina, and other Spanish-speaking countries. So you might have a family on screen with the mother, father, daughter, and son all speaking with different accents. Imagine watching *Gone with the Wind* with Clarke Gable having a Cockney accent, Vivien Leigh having a Boston accent, and Butterfly McQueen sounding like an Aussie. Instead of McQueen saying, 'I don't know nothin' 'bout birthin' babies,' she would have said, 'Bob's your uncle,'"

"Bob's your uncle?"

"Yeah, they say that for everything down there. So you can see how it would be hard to think of them as being in Georgia during the Civil War."

I agreed with her. What choice did I have?

"So," she wrapped up the story, "Hollywood simply took the English versions and dubbed in Spanish. Of course that meant the actors' lip movements didn't correspond with the sound track, but at least they all had the same accent.

"But there's another possibility," she said. "Maybe it's not where he's from. Maybe what he has is not an accent but a lisp or some other speech defect."

"I don't think we say *speech defect* these days."

"Geez. What do we say?"

"I believe the current phrase is *speech challenged*."

"You know how ridiculous that is, Hubert? Speaking isn't challenging unless you have an impairment. What's wrong with telling the truth? My little brother, Mark, is deaf. He's not hearing challenged, and he isn't gifted with a different sort of communication. He's deaf."

Her "little" brother is six feet two inches of muscle and played football at UNM.

"He's amazing," I said. "I knew him for what—about seven years—before I realized he was deaf."

"Yeah. Very few people know he's deaf, and he wants it that way. Mom spent the year after he was born learning oral training techniques. When he was about three, she hired a professional oral trainer. She lived with us until Mark started high school. Eleven years, Hubie. Four hours a day, seven days a week. That's how long Matt had oral training. And now he speaks so clearly that you didn't even know he's deaf."

"And he has a New Mexico accent. So it wouldn't matter if Arcilla were deaf, because we could still tell where he was from by his accent."

She frowned and asked, "Why did you choose 'Arcilla?'"

"Because it means 'clay' in Spanish."

"Clay the name or clay the mud?"

"Clay the mud. Clay is not a first name in Spanish. It is in English of course and its origin is—"

"I know. Someone who worked with clay."

"Right."

16

Arcilla showed up again the next afternoon.

"Welcome back," I said, hoping a friendly greeting might loosen his tongue. "A friend and I were talking about you last evening."

His countenance darkened. "Why were you talking about me?"

"I told her you had an accent, and she wondered what sort of accent it is."

"I do not have an accent."

"Well, maybe you have acquired a slight one without realizing it. Do you speak a language other than Spanish? Sometimes a second language can spill over a bit and give a person a faint accent."

"I speak two languages in addition to Spanish."

Finally we were getting somewhere. "What are they?"

"I'm certain Spanish is the only language we have in common."

We were not getting anywhere. I decided the only way to get information out of Arcilla would be to have him waterboarded at Guantanamo.

Then he surprised me by smiling. "I apologize for being brusque when first we met. The pot you have is a family heirloom. I was upset to see it for sale in your shop."

"Do you have yours with you?"

He nodded and placed it on the counter.

I asked him to wait while I got my pot and placed it next to his. "They appear to be identical, right?"

"Of course."

"Run your finger slowly around the interior of each pot."

He did so. "They are quite different on the inside."

I nodded my agreement. "Yours has an irregular interior surface. That's because potters don't pay much attention to the inside of their clay work unless it's something like a cereal bowl where the interior is visible. But if the wall of the pot turns in like a vase, an urn, or a ginger jar, then the inside is invisible. Your pot has an irregular interior because it is old and made by hand. But my pot has a smooth and uniform interior because it is made by a machine."

"But why do they look identical on the outside, even with regard to small irregularities?"

"Because mine was copied from one like yours. But the copying was not done by a human potter. It was done by a 3-D printer."

He stared at me. "I don't know what that is."

"Neither did I until very recently. The best way I can explain it is that the machine measures all the surface dimensions of an object—height, length, curves, angles, bumps, everything. Then it uses that pattern to create a pot with the exact same surface of the one being copied. But since you can't really see the inside of the pot, there's no reason to copy the inside. The inside of your pot is uneven because the fingers of the potter made it. But the machine makes the inside smooth. The wall thickness is almost exactly three sixteenths of an inch at every point."

"What is three sixteenths of an inch in millimeters?"

"Approximately 4.76."

"How can this machine make such a thin wall of clay?"

"I think that's why it is called a printer. It emits a string of clay soft enough to flow out of the tip of the machine—like ink flows from the stylus of a normal printer. But the clay is firm enough to hold its shape and support the next string and so on."

"It sounds more like a loom than a printer."

"Yes. That's a good analogy. It sort of weaves the clay string into a pot."

He looked dejected as he said, "So your pot is not a family heirloom."

"No. It was made recently. But I'm curious as to why you would have thought it to be a family heirloom. The one you brought here is obviously the family heirloom."

He picked up his pot. "This is not *the* family heirloom. It is *one* of the family heirlooms. My family has a collection of these pots."

"And you wondered how I came to have one."

"Yes."

"I am a potter. I'd be interested in anything you can tell me about the pots."

"It's a long story."

"Would it go well with coffee?"

He nodded.

I turned the sign on the door to *Closed* and led Arcilla back to the living quarters. I brewed a pot of New Mexico Piñon Coffee dark roast.

He took a sip, raised his eyebrows, and said, "I did not think it would be possible to taste such excellent coffee here."

It may be a pottery shop, I thought to myself, *but it's also my house, and I think the coffee I make is a lot better than the factory brew at a Starbucks.*

He sat silent and still for a minute. "My family has lived in the same village in the north on property granted to us by the king in the 17th century. Approximately ten generations ago, a member of the family decided to seek a new life. He was the youngest of five sons and realized his legacy would be small. I suppose he may also have had wanderlust. And there was another reason I will not speak of.

"He was determined to travel to the Far West. Of course in those days, there were no phones or internet. There was not even a reliable postal service. When a family member moved away, many families held a wake—without a body of course—because like death, a move far away usually meant never seeing the person again. When he left, his father gave him one of these pots as a memento.

"So when I saw the picture of your pot in the Albuquerque

newspaper, I assumed you had gotten it from a descendent of the person who left many generations ago. That is why I was so anxious to find out how you acquired the pot."

He took another sip of his coffee, put the cup on the table, extended his legs, and exhaled. And the driven person who had come to my shop three days earlier now looked relaxed. Or maybe just resigned.

I wanted to help him. I said, "I will not tell you how I came to have the copy of the pot. But what I can tell you is that I know the person who made the copy. Call that person X. I know X's family history, and X is not someone descended from your ancestors."

"But where did X get the pot to copy?"

"A person, call him Y, hired X to copy the pot. After X made the copies, he brought this one for me to see because he knew I was in the pottery business."

"Copies?" He seemed alarmed, back to the persona he'd had the first time he came to the shop. "There are more copies?"

"Yes."

"How many?"

"I don't know." I could have told him how many X (Tristan) made, but I had no idea if Y (Nomolos) had made some more.

"Where are they?"

"I don't know that either."

He took a few deep breaths trying to calm back down. "I know you will not reveal the name of X. But can you tell me the name of Y, the person who brought the pot to X to be copied?"

Well, I said I would spare you the story of how I didn't discover what day I was born on until I was almost fifty years old. Unless it became germane to the story of the pots. Which I now think it is.

I grew up in a household of four people: my father, my mother, myself, and my nanny, Consuela Saenz. When I was old enough to think about it, I realized my mother needed a nanny because she was forty-one when I was born and perhaps lacked the energy that women in the normal childbearing age range have. As I grew older, I realized it was also because she was engaged in numerous civic activities which demanded a lot of her time. Despite being busy, my mother was an attentive and kind woman. So was Consuela. I was blessed with two mothers and had a carefree and wonderful childhood.

That narrative changed when I discovered I had a half brother, born to the man who turned out to be my biological father and a woman he had eventually married some time after his involvement with Consuela.

The real story of my household is that when they passed forty, my parents gave up the hope of pregnancy and decided to adopt. Consuela was an unwed pregnant teenager in Silver City, New Mexico. My parents arranged to take care of her medical and living needs, adopt the baby she was carrying, and hire her as a nanny so that she could assist in the raising of her own child.

The CIA could not have done a better job of fabricating a cover story. My father took a leave of absence from UNM, ostensibly to do research. But the real reason was to be away from Albuquerque. They announced to everyone that they were expecting a child. They left out the part about the child they expected already being in Silver City. When they returned a year later, their friends and neighbors assumed they had left before my mother was showing and returned after her tummy had returned to its trim pre-pregnancy state after the birth.

I suspect some of the cattier society women she ran with may have speculated that a post-partum girdle was part of the speedy return of her girlish figure.

When I turned eighteen and enrolled at UNM, Consuela left our household and married Emilio Sanchez. They are a wonderful couple and have a grown daughter named Ninfa. Since my parents died, I continue to see Consuela and Emilio (and Ninfa when she is in town) and think of them as family. I'm certain that neither Emilio nor Ninfa know that Consuela is my birth mother. And I saw no reason to tell them after I discovered it.

Remember my SAP #1? It says any human being can practice any culture. I am a breathing example of a peculiar twist on that SAP. I used to think I was Anglo by birth but also fit into the Mexican-American culture simply because I was surrounded by it in New Mexico. Now I know I am biologically both Anglo and Mexican-American. But it doesn't change anything. I'm not immersed into Mexican-American culture more deeply because I now know my mother is Mexican-American. I was already part of that culture by choice.

Only six people know I'm adopted: Consuela, Sharice, Susannah, Tristan, Whit Fletcher, and Charles Webbe, an FBI Agent.

Consuela is the only one of the six who does not know that I know.

Sharice knows because we have no secrets.

Susannah, Tristan, and the two law enforcement guys know because they are the ones who helped me ultimately figure it out.

So Arcilla wants me to tell him that Nomolos is the person with the original pot from which my copy was made. Nomolos may be a long-lost family member. I don't think I have the right to out him so to speak. What if his parents told him a different story about their background?

I think about all of this and finally hit on a plan. I explain to Arcilla that I don't feel I have the right to tell him who owns the original unless that person gives me permission to do so. I tell Arcilla that—if he wants me to—I will contact the owner of the original, tell him a person came to see the pot and showed me another original identical to the copy. I will tell him that person thinks that the two of them may be from the same family and would like the two of them to meet. If he agrees, then a meeting will be arranged.

Arcilla takes out his handkerchief, dabs his eyes, and thanks me.

I ask him how I can contact him after I talk to the owner of the other original.

"You cannot contact me. I have been staying here in a cheap hotel. I checked out this morning and will look for a better one when I leave here."

"Can I call you?"

"At home, yes. But not while I am travelling." He hands me a piece of paper and says, "Here is my number if you ever need to call me when I am back home."

I fold the paper and put it in my pocket.

So like me, he doesn't have a cell phone. He likes pots. He likes them to be owned by appropriate people. He likes my coffee. I'm beginning to like the guy.

We agree that he will check back in a few days to find out if I've been able to arrange a meeting. We return to the shop, I unlock the door and watch him walk away.

I make a list of things I think I've learned about Arcilla.

1. He has no interests in copies, so he didn't burglarize Tristan's apartment.
2. He doesn't live in Albuquerque because he's in a hotel.
3. But he does live where the *Albuquerque Journal* is distributed. That covers most of New Mexico.
4. He told me his family lives in the north, which makes sense because that's where the king gave land grants.
5. Back in the 17th century, a family member decided to travel to the Far West, probably California.
6. He doesn't have a cell phone.
7. And, much to my surprise, I think hair transplants actually work! As he walked away, I noticed the sort of ring thing separating the hair on the side of his head from the hair on top has almost disappeared.

17

Sharice showed up at two the next afternoon.

"To what do I owe the pleasure of your visit?" I asked.

"Put Geronimo in the patio, close the blinds, turn on the shower, and I'll show you."

I've admitted that I'm seldom described as fit, but I can move quickly when I care to.

I had the front door locked, the sign turned to *Closed*, Geronimo sent to the courtyard, the drapes drawn, my clothes thrown into a corner, and the shower on full blast in two minutes flat.

In the interest of decorum, I will skip ahead to after my heart rate returned to normal. Geronimo was back inside, curled up at the foot of the bed. I was stroking Sharice's slightly extended tummy.

"She just moved," I said.

Sharice laughed and said, "I admire your tenacity. You've stuck with that wacky theory throughout the whole pregnancy."

"According to Dr. Wójcik, it's not wacky."

She smiled and said, "You just stuck with it as an excuse to have sex frequently, not because you wanted a girl."

"I admit it. A girl would be great and so would a boy. And the frequency is because you are irresistible, and also because at my age, I need to make up for lost time."

She giggled. "And I needed to lose my virginity, so it was convenient when you showed up."

When our relationship began to get serious, Sharice insisted that we tell each other about our sexual histories. She made me go first, and it took me about two minutes because I've been womanless most of my life.

Which is no longer a complaint. Being with Sharice makes up for everything.

After I stopped talking, it was her turn. She stared at me silently for about a minute then said, "That's it."

"That's what?"

"That's my sexual history."

Being a virgin was a result of her father's strict upbringing and then not meeting anyone in dental school because it was all study and work, and then getting breast cancer and a mastectomy, after which—it pains me to report—a lot of guys lost interest when she told them.

Men can be so shallow. Myself included on occasion. But not when it comes to Sharice.

But I'm thankful to those clods who failed to pursue her.

Geronimo, as you have likely guessed, is my dog. He looks like a cross between a chow, a collie, and an anteater. Can a cross be between three things? Maybe he's a triangle instead of a cross. It's also a more accurate description because his long neck (the anteater part) hangs down at the same angle as his shaggy tail (the collie part) so he has three sides like a triangle. Except there are only two points of connection instead of three. When it's dark, you can't tell which way he's facing.

He's delighted to be back in the little living quarters behind Spirits in Clay because Sharice's cat is his *bête noir*. Sorry about the French phrase, but I'm trying to learn French which is Sharice's first language because she was born and raised in Montreal. Like Czech, French has a lot of strange marks over the letters, like the little cap over the ê. No wonder English is the world's most widespread language; it's the only one you can type using just the ordinary keys.

The literal meaning of *bête noir* is black beast. Sharice's cat is not black, but he is a beast. He's almost two feet tall, weighs twenty-five pounds and can jump eight feet straight up. Not your ordinary Siamese, Russian Blue, or Ragdoll. Benz is a Savannah cat, a cross between an African Serval and a domestic cat. In this case, his parents must have frequently abstained from sex, because he is not only a male, he is an alpha male, the pecking order among the males in the condo being Benz, me, then Geronimo.

I told her about her father's visit.

"Yeah, he told me. I scolded him, and now I feel guilty about doing so. He looked like a little boy being sent to the corner."

"That's exactly why I'm not worried. His wife died, and you are his only child. You're the most important thing in his life. He is not going to alienate you by refusing to participate in your wedding."

"I told him we are getting married with or without his blessing, so he needs to decide either to go along with what we want or go back home. My baby and my fiancé are the two best things that ever happened to me, and I don't want a downer hanging around."

"Wow. That was sort of rough."

"I know. That's why I feel bad about it."

I took her hand. "It's all going to work out."

"I hope you're right. Remember when he confronted you on his last visit, and you basically called him out. He came back to the condo with a sort of grudging admiration of you. He's always been a stubborn man. A solid and dependable father, but extremely stubborn. Except with my mother; he always deferred to her. You wouldn't know it, but he has a great sense of humor. He used to say, 'Your mother and I discussed the situation and decided to compromise and do it her way.'"

"Sounds like my father. He was a popular teacher at the university, but a man of few words when he wasn't behind a podium. And in all matters other than his work, he deferred to my mother. She decided which events to attend, what shows to see, where to vacation, even the make and model of car to buy. I suspect he liked not having to think about those things."

She laughed and scooted closer to me. "Tell me about your father."

"You already know that he enlisted in the Navy the day after Pearl Harbor and served in the Pacific."

"Right. Where he contracted tuberculosis."

"That wasn't the worst thing that happened to him. He served on the USS *Gambier Bay,* what they called a light aircraft carrier, one of the hundred or so ships involved in the Battle of Leyte Gulf, the largest naval battle in history. It was the first time American ships encountered Japanese suicide attackers, *kamikazes.* One of them flew into the *Gambier Bay.* The ship had a wooden flight deck, and it caught fire when the plane hit it. My father was on flight control duty, which means he was one of those guys you see in old war films who stand on the deck and wave flags at the pilots to signal them to move left or right or higher or lower so that they can land safely on a surface that is pitching and rolling. When the *kamikaze* plane hit the deck, my father was quickly surrounded by the flames."

I smiled as I remembered the next part. "He told me he made a quick inventory of his options: one, wait for help to arrive; two, make a quick sprint through the fire to the part of the deck that was not in flames; and three, jump overboard into the soothing eighty-six-degree water of the Pacific Ocean."

"Let me guess," she said. "He jumped."

"He did. And as he hit the water, the fire reached the refueling tank and blew the deck where my father had been standing about two hundred feet into the air."

"Wow. So jumping saved his life."

"It did. But he thought it was going to end quickly anyway because when he looked up after the explosions, it was raining big chunks of wood."

"And he was lucky that none of them hit him."

"It had nothing to do with luck. He dove down to about thirty feet, and when he came up, the boards were floating harmlessly in the water."

"He could go down thirty feet without scuba equipment?"

"He claimed he had done fifty feet during basic training. He looked like Michael Phelps—tall and muscular with long arms."

"So where did the tuberculosis come in?"

"Sailors on the ship were trying to put out the fire. They had no idea my dad had jumped into the ocean. There was no way to get back onboard, which turned out to be a blessing because the *Gambier Bay* sank. It was the first US carrier to sink in WWII.

"My father swam to shore. But now that I remember it, luck *was* involved. He came ashore in a thick mangrove swamp where no one was around, and no one could get to him without hacking through the mangroves with a machete. But, strangely enough—"

She looked at her watch. "Oops! Got to get back to the condo. Dad's cooking something special."

18

When Tristan returned later than expected to the shop, I told him about Arcilla's second visit and his desire to meet Nomolos.

"No problem," he said in his usual affable voice. "I've got Nomolos' number on my phone. I'll give it to you, and you and Arcilla can work something out with Nomolos."

"Actually," I replied, "there is a problem. I don't want Arcilla to contact Nomolos directly."

"Why?"

"For the same reason I didn't tell Consuela that I know she's my birth mother. I didn't want to throw a monkey wrench into her life. Same goes for Nomolos, even though I don't know him."

"You think Nomolos wouldn't want to meet Arcilla?"

"I don't know. My guess is he'd have no reason not to meet; he might even think it's great to meet someone descended from his family of long ago. But it's not my decision to make. I need to call Nomolos, tell him there's a person who saw the pot in the newspaper and thinks they may be related, and ask him if he wants to meet. If he says no, I can drop it, and Arcilla can't find him. Or if he does find him, it isn't because of me."

Tristan slid his phone from his hip pocket, punched a few buttons, and said, "I'll punch his number, and you can call him."

"No. I can't call him from your number. I don't want you involved."

"Then I'll give you his number, and you can call him from your land line."

"That won't work either. I suspect he may be able somehow to figure out who I am by seeing my number and then linking me to you."

He smiled. "You sound a bit paranoid. But you're right that it wouldn't be hard for almost anyone to connect the dots."

"Almost anyone?"

"Right. But not you. And that's a compliment. You are consistent. But here's what you do—call him from the phone in the art department."

"And say what? 'Hi this is the art department calling you about a person who may be related to you?'"

He laughed and said, "You don't know that the art department got the message about Nomolos, do you?"

I just stared at him.

"Nomolos called UNM's main number and said he wanted to hire someone to help him with a 3-D printer. They told him the two departments most likely to have someone who can do that are computer science and art. So they sent the info to both departments."

"Why didn't I see it?"

"Because you've been skipping out on work."

"I haven't been skipping out. The semester is over. I don't have to go to work."

"Correction: the *faculty* don't have to go to work. Department heads do."

"I'm just interim head. I don't need to do any after-the-semester stuff."

"So why did you go to the graduation meeting?"

"Uhh . . ."

"Exactly."

"How do you know Nomolos' request was forwarded to the art department?"

"Raul Zamoria told me."

Raul was a student in my pottery making class in the fall, the most brilliant person in the class, including the adjunct instructor. I think of him as a potter, but I discovered he's also a computer guy. When I was scrambling to find people to teach, one of the courses with a room full of students but no instructor was Digital Art. Don't ask because I also don't know what digital art is. Not knowing where to turn, I asked the students, and they said try to hire Raul, which I did.

"Why did he call you?" I asked Tristan.

"To tell me about it. He wasn't sure if the request went to computer science, and he wanted me to get a shot at it if I was interested."

"And he wasn't?"

"He works full time for a tech company. They don't mind him teaching an art course on the side, but they own his computer skills; his contract forbids him from doing computer science work for others."

I was about to start cooking when Gladwyn walked in and invited us to dinner. In addition to running F°ahrenheit F°ashions in the space next to Spirits in Clay, he lives in the west third of the building with his new wife, the former Miss Gladys Claiborne.

Miss Gladys—the *Miss* is not technically her first name but might as well be because that's how everyone addresses her—moved to Albuquerque when her husband's doctor suggested the dry climate would be better for him than hot and humid East Texas. Evidently, the climate change didn't help. Mr. Claiborne died, and Miss Gladys has spent the years since his passing gradually reducing her substantial inheritance by operating Miss Gladys' Gift Shop which provides her with both pleasure and red ink, the latter of which she can afford to ignore.

Tristan accepted the invitation before I could think up a reason why we couldn't have dinner with them. So we walked two doors down and sat down to Chicken Enchilasagna.

No, that is not a typo. The dish is alleged to be a cross between enchiladas and lasagna.

Miss Gladys hugged Tristan and said, "Good thing you came. Looks like you've lost a few pounds, but this dish will get them back for you."

"I've been staying with Uncle Hubie."

"Well that explains it. He's probably giving you that vegetarian food his lady friend likes." She turned to me. "You could also use a couple of pounds; those trousers are about to slip off your hips."

I gave her a smile as a response.

"I know you'll like this one because it's half Mexican. And as easy as falling off a log."

One of her favorite metaphors despite the fact that logs are as scarce in Albuquerque as hen's teeth, another of her favorites.

"Just spray oil around the casserole dish and layer in some boneless, skinless, fat-free chicken breasts. Pour in a can of enchilada sauce, sprinkle a package of Kraft shredded cheddar cheese, then a half cup of fresh chopped cilantro, a fourth cup sliced drained black olives, one small can of green chiles, then cover it all up with yellow corn tortillas."

Now you know why residents of Old Town call Miss Gladys *nuestra señora de los casseroles*.

I wondered briefly what sort of chickens produce boneless, skinless, fat-free breasts. The only Italian ingredients were the olives which are not used in traditional Mexican food. I suppose the term *lasagna* applies only to the fact that things are layered. The cilantro was actually curly leaf parsley, but the dish was good if a bit salty.

Gladys and Gladwyn began dating shortly after he opened his shop in Old Town, and they surprised us all by getting married. They are in their late sixties but seem like teenagers with wrinkles.

I like to think that Don Fernando Maria Arajuez Aragon is pleased that the home he built still houses people, but I wonder what he would think of air conditioning and indoor plumbing, not to mention Chicken Enchilasagna.

19

Tristan accompanied me to my office at UNM the next morning.

I dialed Nomolos' number, told him I was the head of the art department, did not give my name, and said we had received the message that he was seeking someone to do some 3-D printing for him, and that is how I knew who he was and also had his telephone number.

"Then an odd thing happened," I told him. "A guy came to me because he saw a picture of your pot in the newspaper. I suppose he came to me because he contacted the university and they told him the info had gone to two departments, and he happened to choose mine, even though we were not involved after that first contact. He wanted to know if I knew how to contact the owner of the pot that was copied. He said his family had a pot identical to that one, and he thought the two of you might be distant cousins or something. I told him I couldn't give out your number without your consent. So I am calling to see if you are interested in meeting with him. If you are, I can give him your number. Otherwise, I will not give anyone your number."

Nomolos and I talked for quite a while before I hung up.

Tristan said, "That was a weird conversation."

"That's because you heard only my half of it," I replied.

He nodded in understanding. "So if I'd heard the whole thing like on a speaker phone, it would have sounded normal, right?"

"Wrong. It would have sounded even weirder."

"So how was it weird?"

"He asked me a bunch of questions about my visitor with the pot, but I kept telling him I didn't know who the visitor was or anything about him except that he said he would return in a couple of days and see if I'd been able to arrange a meeting. Nomolos asked me to describe the visitor. I also refused to do that, saying that I had agreed to one thing and one thing only—to see if both parties were willing to meet. He finally gave up and said he would agree."

"Doesn't sound very weird."

"Right. The weird part came when he explained the only condition under which a meeting can take place."

Tristan smiled. "Does it involve code names and one of them having a black rose in his lapel?"

"No, that would be almost normal. Nomolos wants Arcilla to call him. When he does, Nomolos will give him directions. But Arcilla must make the call from his car."

"Why?"

"Because he is going to give the directions one-by-one, not all at once."

Tristan said, "I don't get it. Why can't Nomolos give the directions one-by-one while Arcilla is sitting on a couch or taking a walk?"

"Because Nomolos wants Arcilla to *carry out* the directions one-by-one, and the directions will be where to drive."

Tristan thought for a moment, then said, "So it would be like 'Drive to Truth or Consequences, then call me.' And then after Arcilla gets to Truth or Consequences and tells Nomolos he's there, Nomolos gives him the next direction which is something like 'Now drive to Cuchillo?'"

"Exactly."

"And the point is?"

"Who knows? So far as I can see, this one-at-a-time system differs from a normal system in just one way. No one will know where Arcilla is except Nomolos."

Tristan's eyebrows rose slightly. "Scary."

"And also not going to happen," I pointed out, "because Arcilla doesn't have a cell phone."

Tristan smiled and said, "I can solve both problems. I'll let Arcilla use one of my cell phones. Then I'll set my own phone to trace the one Arcilla has, so you and I can know where he is at every point in the journey."

"You can do that?"

"Easier than falling off a log," he said and laughed. "I have GPS tracking software on my phone. I can also set up a conference call without Arcilla even knowing it so that we can hear any and all conversations. And maybe keep him safe if anything goes sideways."

Before Tristan left my office to do his work for the registrar, he did a little computer work for me. Using the Banner software, he created a list of all the students in the College of the Arts who were eligible to graduate in June. Then he printed them off on some light blue construction paper I found in the storage closet.

Why light blue? Because I wanted something that would stand out, and it was the only paper in the storage room that met that criterion.

Why was it there? It's an art department; all sorts of things are in there: clay, wood, metal ingots, scary chemicals (those are in a locked cabinet along with knives and other dangerous materials), paint brushes, palette knives (not sharp), rags, paper towels, glues, and odd found objects someone thinks might be useful in a future artwork, which ran the alphabet from an old leather boot to the stump of a willow tree.

Tristan departed and I did the one remaining task since it did not require any technological skills. I used the paper cutter to slice up the blue construction paper in such a way that every name on it was now on its own little rectangle.

The odd thing was that among all the junk in the art department, I couldn't find a sack or box or anything else to dump all the slips of paper into. So I put them in the old boot and went to the dean's office.

20

I made it to Dos Hermanas at 5:00 p.m., where Susannah told me she had a surprise and good news.

The surprise was already on the table, a blue margarita.

She knows I'm a purist. A few years ago she tried to get Angie to make a cucumber jalapeño margarita. Angie stared at her as if Susannah were Father Merrins in *The Exorcist*.

The recipe called for a peeled and seeded cucumber, a seeded jalapeño, lime juice, triple sec, and tequila. You blend it all together then add a drizzle of Grand Marnier. I imagine my Margaritaville Machine could do that easily. It could probably even de-seed the cucumber.

I told her I suspected that recipe came from Santa Fe. No one in the real New Mexico would do anything that fancy.

But I eventually tried it and have to admit it was good.

As a change of pace. Not as my daily tipple.

And now she was touting a new change of pace inspired by the recipe book that came with the industrial strength machine Tristan had given me for my birthday.

This one had tequila, triple sec, Blue Curaçao liqueur, and lime juice. I have to admit it was tasty, but the blue color was off-putting.

"Why are you rolling your eyes up when you take a sip?" she asked.

"Because looking at it makes me feel like I'm drinking one of those ridiculous blue snow cones."

"But you do like the taste?"

"I do. So what's the good news?"

"Remember the most recent course I took on sacred art?"

"Yes. I remember the picture of the crucifix you showed me that had been carved by a woman who was an atheist."

"Germaine Richier. It was for a new Catholic Church being built in France shortly after World War II. It led to a major controversy."

"Couldn't she have guessed that an atheist doing a crucifix might raise an eyebrow or two?"

"Interesting choice of phrasing. Her crucifix didn't have eyebrows because it didn't have a face. It was very abstract because she thought that was the strongest way to depict both the physical and spiritual torment of Christ. The Bishop of Annecy ordered the crucifix to be removed from sight. The church was a pilgrimage church connected with some putative miracles of healing, and most of the attendees were people with injuries, diseases, etc. They loved Richier's crucifix and objected to its removal. They saw in it the suffering they had endured. Eventually the church authorities gave in and allowed the crucifix to be in the church. That event was the catalyst for a great argument about the nature and role of sacred art."

"You also wrote a paper about a Russian icon."

"You *were* paying attention!"

"I was paying *close* attention. I had been accused of murder, in part because of a clue that was in the Cyrillic alphabet."

She smiled. "Cyrillic doesn't have an alphabet, Hubie. It has an алфавит," she said, speaking the Cyrillic letters one at a time just to be funny. Because she learned the basics of the Russian language in an art history course dealing with Russian painters, she knows that the real word in Russian is азбука, derived from the pronunciation of the first two letters of their alphabet. It was her knowledge of Cyrillic that helped me prove I was innocent.

I told her I also remembered the image she showed that looked like a traditional painting of a saint. I couldn't tell if it was a girl or a young boy, but the head was surrounded by a gold halo.

"It wasn't a saint," she said, "although that's what a halo normally signifies. The person in that painting was Tsarevich Dmitry."

"Remind me of the difference between a tsar and a tsarevich."

"*Tsar* means 'king,' and *Tsarevich* means 'prince.' The tsar at that time was Ivan the Terrible, and his son was named Dmitry."

"If the father was known as 'the terrible,' shouldn't the prince have also had some kind of descriptive nickname, like 'Dmitry the Brat?'"

She ignored that and said, "Iconography is present in almost all art, but in religious art it is everywhere. The most obvious ones are the cross representing Christianity, the Star of David for Judaism, and a crescent moon and star for Islam. But others are not so obvious. A lily represents purity, a dog loyalty, a flame life, and a mirror vanity."

"Well of course. Most vanities have a mirror."

"Geez. You want to hear the good news or make bad jokes?"

"Gimme the news."

"I've been invited to give a presentation on religious symbolism in art at a conference. For the first time ever, I feel like a real art historian. Even a real faculty member even though I'm only an adjunct."

"Congratulations. And thanks for making me look good."

She smiled that smile that competes with the desert sun. "Because you chose me as an adjunct, and now you know I deserved it."

"I knew you deserved it then. I already knew you're a scholar. You can even quote Calvin!"

She blushed. "Well, I'm not sure Calvin had much to say about art history. But here's a quote from Hobbes: 'We're so busy watching out for what's just ahead of us that we don't take time to enjoy where we are.' I can guarantee I'm going to take time to enjoy where I am now that I feel like a real art historian."

I have to say I was impressed. First John Calvin and now Thomas Hobbes, author of *Leviathan*, one of the most important works of political philosophy. And they were contemporaries in the 16th century.

Which prompted me to ask her if she was now specializing in 16th-century art, but she said her specialty continues to be symbolism, especially religious symbolism.

Then I remembered she had loved the film *The Da Vinci Code* in which Tom Hanks played Robert Langdon, a symbolist who constantly uncovers the meanings of ancient symbols in the storyline.

I thought it was because she thought Tom Hanks was hot. But I guess she really did like the symbolic stuff.

21

I was about halfway through *Sky Determines* the next day when Collin Clarke came to Spirits in Clay for the third time and asked me if reading about his church had generated any interest on my part about becoming a Seventh-day Adventist.

"I enjoyed learning a bit about your church. I like the fact that you do not believe in predestination."

"Then you should convert because Anglicans do believe in predestination."

"Most Anglicans today do *not* believe in predestination, although I suppose there are some who do."

"I am disappointed," he said, "but I am not surprised. And I am certain that Sharice will not change. So though it pains me to say so, it is perhaps better if the two of you attend services together." Then he smiled and said, "Perhaps you can convince the priest at your church to hold a Saturday night service?"

I laughed and said, "Sharice told me you have a good sense of humor. I will ask the priest. I don't think it matters when people set aside time for fellowship, prayer, and meditation, so Fridays would be fine with me."

"It does matter. God directs us to honor the Sabbath and keep it holy."

"I'm aware of that. But unfortunately, there is no way for we humans to know what day is the Sabbath."

"Why do you say that?"

"The Bible says that God created the universe in six days, and on the seventh day he rested."

He nodded.

"Bear with me," I said. "I'm a mathematician at heart, and so my analysis will be based on that rather than scripture. But it will be consistent with scripture. If we number all the days in the history of the universe, the Sabbaths will all be multiples of seven. The first Sabbath was day seven, when God rested. The second Sabbath was day fourteen. The third Sabbath was day twenty-one. The fourth Sabbath was the twenty-eighth day of the young universe, and so on. Am I correct?"

"Yes."

"So the only way to tell if any day is a Sabbath is to see if it is a day whose number in the list of all the days of the universe is multiple of seven. But how can we know the number of any day? God would know. But how would a human know? No human being started counting the days of the universe at the very beginning. Scripture contains that fact by inference because it says in Genesis that God created Adam and Eve on the sixth day. So no human started counting at day one."

"Perhaps God told Adam and Eve what day was the Sabbath, and they passed it along over the centuries."

"Yes, that might have happened," I said. "But it's difficult to imagine that the count has remained accurate, especially in light of all the calendar changes instituted by humans. So last Friday at sundown, you believe a Sabbath began. Which means the number of that day was a multiple of seven. But was it the seventh million day of the universe, the fourteenth million day, the 777th billion day? I do not believe anyone can answer that question."

"God knows the answer."

"Indeed. But we do not."

"Religious belief is not based on mathematics."

"True. But God gave us a brain. So He must expect us to use it."

"The Jews have been honoring the Sabbath from the beginning. My church simply follows their path."

"But you disagree with the Jews about what happens when a person dies. So you adopt some beliefs of Judaism and reject others. If they are wrong about what happens when you die or any other religious concept, then they are fallible. And if they are fallible, then they may also be wrong about the Sabbath."

He smiled and said, "You might almost be taken for a modern-day Pharisee."

"Except I don't have their 'holier than thou' attitude. At least I hope I don't. I question not to belittle but to understand."

"I've enjoyed our conversation," he said. "I will think more about it."

22

I went to my office at UNM the next morning and found a note from Jane Robinson pinned to my door.

Ms. Robinson is the administrative assistant to Dean Gangji. Her blue eyes and personality are both warm and friendly.

I walked to her office.

"Stand over there," she said, pointing to a clothes rack on wheels, and she came out from her desk to the rack and pulled a graduation gown off a clothes hanger.

"Try this on."

I did and she correctly noted that it was too long. I'm 5'6" so "It's too long" is a phrase I both hear and utter frequently.

The next one was also too long, but it was the shortest one on the rack, so she told me to take it.

Then I tried a few mortar boards until we got one the right size.

I assumed that was the end of my fitting session, but she then handed me a graduation hood. They are called hoods because at some point back in the Middle Ages, monks wore them over their heads. Modern day faculty wear them hanging on their back outside of the robe. The colors of the hood are from the university that granted their degree. The hood Ms. Robinson handed me was cherry with silver trim, the colors of the University of New Mexico.

"This is a nice hood," I said, "but I can't wear it."

"Of course you can. Hoods don't have to fit."

"They don't have to fit physically, but they have to fit symbolically. I have an undergraduate degree in accounting from UNM, but I do not have a graduate degree."

She waved a hand through the air. "I know that. I'm the one who helped you fill out all the employment forms. But the graduation procession would look strange if one of the department heads didn't have a hood. So the dean directed me to give you one and tell you to wear it."

"So it's sort of like my becoming interim department head."

She laughed and said, "Exactly. You didn't ask for that job, and you didn't ask for this hood."

"More to the point," I said, "I'm not qualified for either one."

She tried to keep a straight face, but a slight smile was peeking out when she said, "It's not for you or me to decide. The dean decides who is qualified for what."

I gathered my regalia and walked back to Spirits in Clay.

23

Tristan is the calmest person I know. He could be the "after" guy in an ad for tranquilizers.

But I could tell he was agitated when I got back to the shop where I'd left him in charge.

"You won't believe what happened. A guy walked in this afternoon and tried to buy the little pot I made for you."

I said the first thing that came to mind: "Arcilla?"

Which didn't make sense. If it had been Arcilla, Tristan would not have said "A guy."

"It wasn't Arcilla. He was a lot younger, maybe around my age. But he did look familiar."

"The delivery guy who brought you the 3-D printer and stuff?"

"No, that guy was about your age."

"Maybe Arcilla's son?"

He thought about it for a moment. "No. He didn't resemble Arcilla."

"Nomolos' son."

"I never saw Nomolos."

"Oh. Right." The shock of another person wanting to buy the little pot had jumbled my reasoning.

"Did he say why he wanted the pot?"

"Not at first. But when I refused to sell it to him, he became more demanding and told me his family owns the rights to that design and could sue me for infringing on their copyright. Is that true?"

"I don't know much about copyright law, but being as how Nomolos asked you to make copies of the pot, I don't see how you as copier could be guilty of copyright infringement."

"He also said that it was extremely important that no one else has copies, but he wouldn't say why. The guy seemed a bit scary."

"You think he might return?"

"It wouldn't surprise me. And he might do it when he thinks no one is here."

"To steal the pot?"

"Maybe. There must be something about the little pot we've missed or overlooked, something that makes people want it."

"Did you show him the pot?"

"No. I didn't want to go to the back and open the secret hiding place while he was alone in the shop."

"You thought he might grab a pot and run?"

"Yes. Not because he wanted to steal a pot but because he might do so with the idea of offering to return it in exchange for the little one."

I left Tristan in the shop and retrieved the little pot.

We both stared at the thing hoping to see something we had missed.

"The design lines," he finally said.

"What about them?"

"Maybe they're a secret code."

"Like in *The Da Vinci Code*," I replied.

"Exactly."

The design looked more or less like this: ה"ב ה"ב ה"ב except instead of being lined up, the motif curved around the opening like decorations around a round window.

"Looks like maybe Arabic calligraphy," said Tristan.

"Susannah!" I said.

Tristan gave me a strange look. "The design is a circular repetition of the Arabic spelling of 'Susannah?'"

"No. But she's an expert on symbolism in art. In fact, she's been invited to give a presentation on the topic at an academic conference."

"So let's get her to look at it," he said. Then he thought for a moment and said, "I think I know what she'll tell us."

"Really?"

"Yes. In *The Da Vinci Code*, the Robert Langdon character played by Tom Hanks looks at the painting of *The Last Supper* and discovers that sitting to the right of Jesus is not the apostle John as is commonly believed, but it is Mary Magdalene instead. And also the famous cup from which Christ allegedly drank, the Holy Grail, is conspicuously left out of the painting. Then Langdon spouts some weird theory that the Holy Grail—which medieval knights were fixated on finding—was not a cup at all but was Mary Magdalene herself who was married to Jesus. So she was the human receptacle for Jesus' blood line. Then he says that Da Vinci's *Mona Lisa* is a symbol for the sacred feminine."

I was stunned by Tristan's detailed recall of the film. *Good to be young* ran through my mind. I was amazed he could remember the details of a film that came out when he was a teenager. "So you're saying that maybe this little bowl was not a candle at all but was maybe used to take wine for communion?"

"Exactly."

"And the decorations?"

"I'm guessing they aren't decorations," he said. "I think they may be letters of the Aramaic language Jesus spoke. Maybe it's Jesus as spelled in Aramaic."

I stared at him. "Amazing. I don't have a clue whether your theory is correct, and it seems way too unlikely to be true. But it does make a weird sort of sense."

"And we were talking about why this little pot might be valuable," he said. "Well, maybe it's the most valuable thing in human history—the Holy Grail. Not the human one that Langdon says is Mary Magdalene, but the actual one Jesus drank from the night before he was crucified."

"But that cup is not in the painting."

"Right. But his sharing bread and wine is in the scriptures. So there had to be a cup. And this could be it."

"Now you've gone way over the top. You made this thing a couple of weeks ago. It is *not* the Holy Grail."

He smiled, and I could see he was undeterred. "But it could be a copy of it."

24

I usually walk to the university, but it was way too hot to walk in a gown, and carrying it along with the hood and mortar board would be awkward.

So I drove. I knew parking would be at a premium for the graduation ceremony, but as department head, I have a reserved space.

Which contained a sedan from which were emerging a nice-looking couple and a young woman in a gown who was, judging from the smiles on the couples' faces, their daughter.

I couldn't bring myself to ask them to find another space. I double-parked just long enough to take my graduation apparel into my office, and then I drove to Tristan's apartment and parked in his space since he was still staying in the shop with me and had no need of the spot at his apartment.

I walked back to UNM, retrieved my apparel and went to the old Johnson Gym on the campus. Graduations at UNM are normally held at the University Arena, a.k.a. The Pit, which is about a mile south of the main campus and has tons of parking. But it was undergoing some repairs, and since there is no other space large enough to handle the graduation (other than the football stadium which is hardly appropriate), the administration had decided to have the colleges hold separate ceremonies in smaller spaces. Three of the colleges would hold graduations in the old Johnson Gym at

9:00 a.m., noon, and 3:00 p.m. The College of the Arts had drawn the short straw; i.e., 9:00 a.m.

The awarding of the undergraduate degrees for The College of the Arts took just over an hour. Two imposters had attempted to join the line of graduates, but we'll never know what hijinxs they had in mind because they didn't have one of the blue construction paper strips with their name on it, and they were escorted out of the building by the university police.

There was a brief interlude between the awarding of the undergraduate and graduate degrees during which two things took place. The first was that a small ensemble of musicians from the UNM Band played uplifting music.

The second thing that happened was, so far as I know, unprecedented in the history of the University. Dean Gangji pulled me aside, thanked me for the idea of the blue slips of paper, and told me to take off my hood and get in the line of students about to be awarded graduate degrees.

I stared at him blankly.

He held out his hand. "Give me the hood."

I did so. He would make a good Marine Corps drill sergeant.

"Get in line."

I did that, too.

What followed is blurred in my memory, but it included someone showing me where I was to be in the line, hearing my name called, walking up to the dean who put my hood on and shook my hand. Then there were raucous yells and applause. I looked into the audience as I went down the stairs from the makeshift stage and saw Tristan, Susannah, Freddie, Sharice and her father, Gladwyn and Miss Gladys, Martin, Consuela, Emilio, and Angie from Dos Hermanas.

I know what happened next because I was told about it later, but I don't actually remember it because I was unconscious. I stepped on my gown and fell down the stairs.

25

All the gang who saw me fall were at Dos Hermanas that night to celebrate my receiving a Master of Fine Arts degree from UNM. I still suspected my getting that degree was either a hoax or a prank, but I said nothing because Dean Gangji was also with us at Dos Hermanas.

And also because the bandage on my lower lip made saying anything painful.

Dean Gangji and Collin Clarke had decided to sit together after they were introduced, perhaps because they both have religious objections to alcohol. Gangji ordered tea; Clarke ordered orange juice.

Angie was seated as a guest, and Guadalupe from the kitchen had been pressed into service as a server.

Gladwyn had his usual pink gin, about which the less said the better, and Miss Gladys was enjoying a Pimm's Cup: two ounces of Pimm's No. 1, and four ounces of lemonade with a mint leaf garnish. The longer she's with Gladwyn, the more she indulges in British cocktails, and the longer he's with her, the more he enjoys her casseroles. I can't decide which one is benefitting least, but they are deliriously happy.

Consuela was having *horchata* and Emilio was drinking a Tecate. Tristan and Martin were also having Tecates. Susannah and

Freddie were drinking Gruet. I wondered if it was in celebration of something.

Angie was sipping a five-year-old tequila *añejo*, the five years of aging in this case having taken place in charred barrels that had been used to age bourbon.

I love that stuff, but can't manage the sipping part, so I stuck with my traditional margarita. No jalapeños. No cucumbers.

Dean Gangji tapped his teacup with a spoon and said, "A toast to our newest MFA—Master Hubert Schuze!"

Everyone added "hear, hear" or some other cheer of support, and there was a good deal of glass clinking.

When that settled down, the dean announced there was a meeting of the department heads in the morning at 8:00 a.m., advised me not to have a second drink so that I'd have a clear head for the meeting, then said his goodbyes.

Susannah and Freddie left shortly thereafter. I really wasn't trying to spy on them, but it was impossible not to notice that they were headed toward his temporary sleeping location of F°ahrenheit F°ashions.

Gladwyn and Miss Gladys were next to go, claiming that old age required them to bed down early, but I thought I detected a look in their eyes unrelated to sleep.

Consuela and Emilio said they were staying to order a light meal.

Angie finished her tequila añejo and resumed her server duties. Tristan announced he wanted to return to his apartment for the first time since it had been burgled and that Martin was going to stay there for the night to avoid the long trip back to the Rez. And probably, though he didn't say so, to be with Tristan in case the bandits made a return visit.

Then Collin Clarke stood up, kissed his daughter on the cheek, and said, "I'm going back to the loft. See you two lovebirds tomorrow."

Sharice and I watched him walk away.

I looked at her. "Was this whole day a set-up or what?"

"Maybe," she said. "But either way let's take advantage of it."

26

Despite my sore lip, we did what you suspected we would do at the back of my shop.

Then I let Geronimo in and we talked.

Sharice and I that is. Geronimo simply yawned.

"My father has given in gracefully," she said.

"Indeed he has. I'm growing to like him. I assume he'll participate in our wedding?"

"Yes, but with a few provisos. First, he doesn't want us to get married on the Sabbath. Second, he doesn't want alcohol, pork, or shellfish served at the reception."

"I'm willing to go hungry and thirsty for as long as I have to if he'll be in the wedding."

"I'm so happy. I really thought he might refuse, but his talks with you seem to have softened him. He said you talked about religion."

"We did. We didn't agree on details of doctrine, but we did agree on some larger issues. But mainly we both talked and we both listened."

"So shall we set a date?"

"How about tomorrow," I said.

"Get serious."

"I am serious. I want us to be married before our daughter is born."

"The birth of our *child* is months away. But maybe we should do it soon and save Dad a second trip."

"How long is he planning to be here?"

"He has an open-end return ticket. He can run his business from here without too much difficulty, but I think he'd like to get back by the end of the month. Let's do it in June!"

"How about letting your dad choose the date?"

"Great idea. I can't tell you how happy I am."

"Me, too."

She paused. "I just regret that your parents didn't live to see you get married."

"I think they knew I'd get married. Eventually. They knew I did everything later than most people, so they probably aren't surprised that it didn't happen until I was fifty."

"Tell me the rest of the story about your father in the Philippines."

"First let me tell you about Ross Calvin."

"You mean John Calvin?"

"No. Ross. Unrelated so far as I know. But Ross was also a cleric. Ross Calvin and my father had a lot in common. Each lived most of his life in New Mexico. They both had respiratory problems. They were both cured in Silver City. They both had PhDs. They were both Episcopalians. My father taught history of the Southwest and consulted Ross Calvin's books and papers for background. Ross Calvin's papers are in The Center for Southwest Research, which is part of the UNM Library. My father had a dog-eared copy of Ross Calvin's *Sky Determines* on his bookshelf. Since he never bought used books, the dog-earing came from my father."

"So Ross Calvin was a historian?"

"No. His doctorate was in philology. But after he came to New Mexico, he tried to learn everything about his new home. He studied our history, our people, our geology, flora and fauna."

"So I imagine he was obviously a great source of information for your father."

"Yes. But there is one thing about him that puzzles me. Like his namesake, John Calvin, Ross Calvin believed in predestination.

But according to his biographer, Ross was bitter at God about his first wife's death and his second wife's descent into madness."

"Understandable. Coping with that would test anyone's faith."

"But it doesn't make sense if everything is determined."

"Making sense is rational, Hubie. But emotions are also human, and you can't always make sense of them."

"I think there should be a logical explanation for everything."

"But if there's an explanation for everything," she replied, "then maybe that means determinism is true."

I smiled and said, "Now my head is hurting."

"So shut up about philosophy and tell me the story. You know the one I mean. It's a real cliff-hanger. At the end of the first episode, Dudley Doright Schuze jumped off a flaming ship, dived deep into the Pacific to avoid razor-sharp pieces of the ship raining down from above, made his way back to the surface, and swam fifty miles to shore where he ended up marooned alone in a mangrove swamp."

"Exactly," I joked. "Except it was more like two miles rather than fifty, and he wasn't alone for long. A Japanese soldier stumbled into the same little clearing between the roots of the trees."

"Well the soldier obviously didn't kill your father, but it must have been awkward to say the least."

"You ever read *All Quiet on the Western Front*?" I asked.

That question changed the tone of the conversation.

"That was the most depressing thing I ever read," she said, "and yet I couldn't put it down. I even watched the old film. Remember that scene when the German soldier Paul is separated from his company and forced to hide in a shell hole and then a French soldier jumps into the shell hole with him, and Paul instinctively stabs him?"

I nodded and said, "Paul has to watch as the guy dies a slow and painful death. After the French soldier dies, Paul looks through his things and finds that his name was Gérard Duval and that Duval had a wife and child at home. I thought the story would end with Paul looking up the wife after the war and apologizing."

"I was not that optimistic," she said. "The book was pure misery. There was no way to pin a moment of happiness on its tail. I hope you father's story isn't like that one."

"It isn't. It does have two enemies thrown together, but in a mangrove swamp instead of a shell hole. And like Paul and Gérard, they realized they were not really enemies. The soldier who wandered into the mangrove was a Filipino who had been conscripted by the occupying Japanese Army. He may have been a deserter. If so, who could blame him? The Japanese had invaded and overrun his country. Why should he serve in their army? My father said he seemed to be on the verge of starvation. He was bony, weak, and collapsed at my father's feet.

"As background," I said, "mangroves are the foundation of an ecosystem that generates a productive food web. As the leaves fall into the water and decay, they provide nutrients for various invertebrates and algae. The invertebrates and algae serve as food for small organisms such as sponges, jellyfish, shrimp, and young fishes. My dad fed the Filipino raw shrimp and fish. I guess you could say they dined on sushi. And dad collected rainfall and dew in his inverted helmet, so they had fresh water to drink. After a day or two when the guy was strong enough to speak, he told my father his name was de la Cruz.

"The battle ended three days later, and by then de la Cruz was able to stand. The American ships came closer to land as they prepared to put soldiers on the island to pursue the Japanese troops who were retreating. My father waded out into the shallows and yelled and waved his hands until someone noticed him. They sent a lifeboat after him and he made them wait while he lifted de la Cruz above the mangrove's roots and carried him out into the shallows. They were taken to a hospital corpsman who said de la Cruz had tuberculosis. My father wasn't showing any symptoms, but they sent him back to Hawaii where the doctors confirmed he had it as well, and that was the end of his active service. You already know the part about his recovery in Silver City at the Veterans Hospital."

"Did he ever find out what happened to the guy?"

"Yes. He died. But before he did, he wrote a letter to my father and gave it to a corpsman who gave it to his commanding officer, and which somehow eventually reached my father in Silver City. That letter was among the things I ran across when I emptied the house. It was a touching letter. De la Cruz told my father he was dying from tuberculosis, but he was thankful that he was in a clean hospital with good care and was able to see his family. He told my father he had directed his teenage daughter to name her firstborn son after my father."

"Wow. Did that come to pass?"

"I don't know. But I do know that my father reciprocated when he named me."

She stared at me for a few seconds. "De la Cruz's first name was Hubert."

"Close. It was Uberto. He was named after Uberto Crivelli."

"Who is Uberto Crivelli?"

"Pope Urban III."

"So you're named after a pope?"

"Yep. I'm probably one of the few people named after a pope who isn't Catholic."

"Pope Urban III wasn't Catholic?" she said and laughed at my fractured syntax. "But the Philippines are a Catholic nation, right?"

"Right. The Philippines were a Spanish colony for over three centuries. Spain ceded the colony to the US in 1898 after losing the Spanish-American War. But the residents didn't suddenly stop being Catholic or stop speaking Spanish just because Spain lost the war. Filipinos who were in their forties when World War II began would have grown up speaking Spanish. That's why de la Cruz and my father could communicate. My dad spoke Spanish."

"Do they still speak Spanish in the Philippines?"

"Some do. Spanish remained one of their official languages until the law was changed back in the 1980s. Today there are only two official languages, Filipino and English."

"What happened to Tagalog?"

"It's still tagging along."

She rolled her eyes.

I said, "What was called Tagalog is now called Filipino, and it now also includes some words from some of the lesser known languages spoken there. Only about five percent of Filipinos speak Spanish these days. So the irony is that Spanish gradually disappeared from the Philippines after we took it over, but it grew so much here that more people now speak it in the US than in the Philippines."

27

The meeting of the department heads the next morning was actually at 9:00 a.m. Dean Gangji told me 8:00 a.m. because he wanted to speak to me alone before the meeting but didn't want me to worry all night about why the dean of the college wanted to see me.

Jane Robinson brought coffee to the dean's inner office then closed the door behind her when she left.

After a bit of small talk about last night at Dos Hermanas, Gangji said he wanted to explain why I had been granted a Master of Fine Arts, usually just called an MFA.

"There are actually two explanations," he said, "one which explains the justifications, and one that explains the reasons. I'll begin with the justifications. An MFA requires sixty credits of coursework at the graduate level including credit for an art project which is basically the MFA version of a thesis. If the MFA is in music, for example, the student may be required to compose a symphony or a requiem. The coursework for an MFA is unlike the coursework for a Master of Arts degree in something like history where the courses are generally lecture courses with written exams. It's also unlike the coursework for a Master of Science degree in something like chemistry where the courses usually involve lab work.

"Most of the courses for an MFA do not involve classwork, written exams, or laboratories. They involve creative work: composing music, painting, playing an instrument, sculpting, dancing, acting, creating theater sets, etc."

He handed me a paper. "This is a list of the work that earned you an MFA."

Since I never took an art course in my life, I was not surprised that the paper was blank.

I was staring at it when the dean said, "Turn it over."

It had this list:

Class	Credit
ART 1050: Pottery Methods (transferred from Feats of Clay)	6
ART 1115: Pre-Columbian Art (transfer of Archaeology 1115)	6
ART 1125: Art Preservation (transfer of Archaeology 1125)	6
ART 1227: Artifact Classifications (transfer of Archaeology 1227)	6
ART 1345: Museum Studies (transfer of Archaeology 1345)	6
ART 1378: Southwestern Art (transfer of Archaeology 1378)	6
ART 1450: Art Restoration (PLA)	6
ART 1499: Art Business (PLA)	12
ART 1499: MFA Project	Total: 60

I stared at it. I looked up at him.

"Do you have any questions?" he asked.

"Why are those archaeology courses listed?"

"They are courses you took when you were in the archaeology program."

"I didn't finish that program."

"Right. But you passed those courses. So we transferred the credits to art since the courses dealt with pottery which is your area of art."

"What does PLA stand for?" I asked.

"It stands for prior-learning assessment. It's what colleges and universities do to award college credit for a student's nonacademic experiences and training."

"What nonacademic experiences have I had that qualify me to receive credit in art restoration and art business?"

"You've run a successful art business for years, and you have restored many pots in the process."

"How can you transfer credits from Feats of Clay? It's just a pottery studio that teaches pot-making for a fee."

"Some of their teachers have worked here as adjuncts. You got the same training from them you would have gotten from us."

There were probably other questions I should have asked, but I couldn't think of any.

After a few moments of silence that indicated I was out of questions, Gangji said, "Now I want to explain the reasons we wanted you to have a graduate degree. You serving as department head with only a baccalaureate was unusual. But we justified it based on the fact that the position came open at the last moment."

Right, I thought. *When Shorter was shot to death in his office.*

"But," he continued, "we cannot use that excuse for the summer and fall. And yet, the situation remains essentially the same. You are still the only person a majority of the faculty will support for the position. And you are the only one I would support except for Helga Ólafsdóttir, Harte Hockley, and Ann Abeyta, all of whom are unwilling. Thus, I want you to continue as interim department head for the summer and fall. As I said, you handled the job well. But the fact is we have no other viable choices."

I shook my head. "There is another viable choice. Frederick Blass would get the support of most of the faculty, and unlike me, he has a doctoral degree and years of experience in the job."

"He also has a prison record. It is one thing to hire him to teach; quite another to put him in charge of the department."

I opened my mouth, but he showed me his palm. "I like Freddie as much as you do. But he will not be department head."

He stood. "It's time for the meeting. Come along so I can announce to your colleagues that you are continuing for the summer and fall."

28

When I got back to Spirits in Clay, Tristan had the same look on his face that he had the last time he minded the shop.

And for the same reason.

"Yet another person came in today and asked about the little pot."

"Unbelievable. I'm beginning to think your suggestion that I buy a 3-D printer and we start making and selling these things is a good idea."

"Except this person didn't want to buy it. She just wanted information."

"What information?"

"Wait 'til you hear this. It's bizarre. She claims to be the sister of the young guy who tried to buy it."

"Claims to be?"

"She doesn't look like him."

"Did she give you her name or her brother's name?"

"No."

"So what information did she want?"

"She wanted me to tell her—quote—'everything he said.'"

"What did you tell her?"

"I told her it would be unethical for us to make public what our customers say to us."

"Good answer. And it also has the benefit of being true."

"Then I asked her why she didn't just ask her brother, and she said they weren't on very good terms. Then she said if I wouldn't tell her what her brother said, could I at least tell her what I knew about the pot. I didn't want to lie to her, but I was afraid I might mess things up by letting her know I was the guy who made the copies, so I told her I was just a hired hand, and if she wanted information about the pot, she'd have to talk to the owner."

"You did the right thing. There's no need to tell her you made the copies."

"Yeah. She's not someone I'd want to upset," he said and gave me a smile that was seeking a question.

So I asked it. "Why is she not someone you'd want to upset?"

"Because there was a pistol in her purse."

"She pulled a pistol on you?"

"No. But it was a big baggy purse and easy to see into. And I wondered if she didn't leave it hanging open just so I'd see the gun. I tried not to stare at it, but it's possible she noticed that I noticed."

"Then what happened?"

"She said she'd come back and talk to the owner. Sorry."

I thought about it briefly. "If she does, maybe I can learn something from her about my pot and all its little brothers and sisters."

"Like what?"

"I have no idea. Maybe I could at least find out who she is."

"Maybe the police can do that."

"I don't see how. Unless her picture is in the NCIC files."

He smiled. "Or her fingerprints."

"Fingerprints?"

"Yes. Because she placed her hand on the counter when she first came in."

We called Whit Fletcher. He brought a lab tech who lifted the fingerprints off the counter.

"Good thing you keep this here wood countertop so clean," Whit said. "Normally glass or metal surfaces are the easiest ones to lift a print from, but your wood is as slick as glass."

"I keep it that way," I said.

"Why not? You don't have much else to do what with the small number of customers you get."

"Quality is more important than quantity."

"A woman with a pistol in her purse don't count as a quality customer, Hubert."

I told him I agreed with him and showed him the pictures of her as she came in and left. The lab tech transferred them from my laptop to a little stick thing that he attached to the laptop and then removed.

"If her prints or picture are on file anywhere, we'll know who she is."

I hit myself on my forehead and told Whit we'd had two other people wanting the same pot, and I hadn't thought about fingerprints.

"Why should you have? Were they toting pistols?"

"I don't think so. But they could have been the people who broke into Tristan's apartment."

Whit shook his head. "Wouldn't help. They ran down all the prints in his apartment, and they all belonged to people on the list Tristan gave 'em."

I had the lab tech guy examine the little pot for prints. He said there were prints on the inside but they weren't useful because the fingers had not just been pressed onto the pot, but had been slid along which made them impossible to identify. But there were good ones on the outside.

I remembered asking Arcilla to feel the inside of the pot, and he ran his finger around it. I was holding it as he did so. So the good prints were mine.

29

Arcilla came in the next morning.

I called Tristan, told him Arcilla was in the shop, and asked him to bring the phone.

While we waited, I gave Arcilla an abbreviated version of how he would meet person X.

Or maybe we were calling him Y at that point. It doesn't matter. The main thing is we weren't calling him Nomolos, and I wasn't telling Arcilla anything at all about the guy with the letter for a name except for the fact that he had the pot and was willing to meet.

Arcilla reminded me he did not have a phone that would work in a car. I told him I also didn't have such a phone but that my nephew was bringing one for him to use.

Tristan arrived and showed Arcilla how to use the phone. We walked outside to Arcilla's car, and he got behind the wheel. Tristan had entered Nomolos' telephone number into the phone and had it showing on the screen.

Tristan looked at me and said, "Tell him to tap that top number, and the guy he is meeting will answer. Tell him if there is any problem with the phone along the way to tap the other number which is my number, and I'll try to fix it."

I translated for Arcilla.

We watched him tap the number and then converse, nodding. He gave us a thumbs up and drove away.

I told Tristan what had been said.

We walked back into Spirits in Clay where Susannah was waiting because of course she wanted to participate in what she thought might turn out to be a murder mystery. Or maybe already was.

Tristan had brought her along, but she had stayed in his car until Arcilla left because we didn't want Arcilla wondering why yet another person was involved.

I turned the sign to *Closed* and locked the door. Tristan placed two phones on the counter. The first one had a map on the screen, and we saw an icon of a car moving along Rio Grand Boulevard and then turning right onto Interstate 40 East. A few minutes later it went through the cloverleaf of Interstates 40 and 25 and ended up headed north on 25.

"Did he seem nervous about getting the instructions one at a time and therefore not knowing where he's going until he gets there?" Tristan asked.

"Not in the least. He said my being able to arrange a meeting was a sign from God, and that he was anxious to meet his long-lost family member."

We watched the car continue north. It was in the slow lane and travelling well below the speed limit. I imagined he was getting a few honks and frowns from the other drivers. There must be some chemical in the asphalt used for interstates that saps manners out of people.

As the car approached Santa Fe, the phone rang, and I was relieved that we could hear the conversation. Even though I know Tristan is a tech wizard, I can't seem to convince myself that this stuff is possible.

The conversation was brief. Nomolos told Arcilla to take Highway 84/285 north towards Espanola. Arcilla did so and was therefore continuing north and a bit west.

Of course, Arcilla didn't know the caller was Nomolos. In fact, neither did we. We had good reason to *believe* it was Nomolos, but we couldn't be certain. Nomolos had gone to great lengths to keep people in the dark, so for all we knew someone else was doing the talking under his direction.

The odds that this was the case seemed to increase when Tristan said, "The caller's voice seems familiar."

"Can you put a name to it?"

"Not yet. Maybe when we hear him on the next call."

Nomolos and Arcilla were speaking Spanish of course. Arcilla still had that accent, and the other guy—Nomolos or not—sounded like the average New Mexico Spanish speaker.

Susannah said to Tristan, "Maybe it would help if you imagined that same voice in English."

Tristan and I stared at her.

"Think about it, Tristan," she said. "You don't speak Spanish. So just listen to the tone and stuff. Don't get caught up in the meaning. Treat it like music."

"Actually, that makes sense," said Tristan, and he played back the three conversations which of course he had recorded. "I still can't place it, but listening to it as sound alone seems to help."

The next call came as Arcilla approached the point where Highways 84 and 285 diverge. He was told to take 285 to Ojo Caliente and then wait there for the next call.

Of course we began immediately to speculate about why Arcilla had to stop and wait in Ojo Caliente instead of taking the call as he moved along. It seemed a bit late to suddenly start worrying about New Mexico's hands-free law.

But when we saw the icon of the car stop moving and then listened to the call, we understood. The caller could not give Arcilla a road number because the dirt road he was told to follow had no number. He had to make a few turns at landmarks to get onto the road. Once he had done that, the call ended.

And Susannah and I stared at each other wide-eyed and said in unison: "La Reina!"

30

Tristan stared at me. "Where you got into a bar fight?"

"It was not a bar fight. In fact, I was trying to *avoid* a bar fight."

"Right. And in the process, you knocked a guy unconscious."

"I slipped because I had a cast on, and when I fell the cast hit him in the head."

He turned to Susannah. "And it's where you met Baltazar."

"And spent a lot of time driving back and forth when we were dating."

"What happened, if you don't mind telling me?"

"Simple as one, two, three. One, we liked each other. Two, we got tired of the long drives. Three, neither of us wanted to move."

Tristan turned to me. "You almost got killed up there."

I looked at Susannah. "I would have been except you shot the guy who was about to kill me. He's in prison and will be eligible for parole in just a few years. I may move to the Gila Wilderness if they let him out."

The Cliff's Notes version of the La Reina story is that a guy named Álvar Nuñez brought a pot shard into my shop and told me if I bought it, he would tell me where it came from, a place that might have some valuable old buried pots.

Digging in the cliff dwelling he told me about did not turn up any valuable pots. It did turn up a dead body. I assumed it was one of the original inhabitants, now mummified by time. Susannah thought it was a modern-day murder victim. She was right. When we went to La Reina to try to clear things up, no one in town had ever heard of Álvar Nuñez. Turns out they all knew him. But to them he was Father Jerome, the local Catholic priest. Álvar Nuñez was his name before he entered the priesthood.

If Nomolos lived in La Reina, Father Jerome would know him.

The phone with the icon of the car was now moving cross country. At least it appeared that way because the dirt road it was on was not known to the map in the phone's software.

When the car stopped, we heard the phone in it ring. Nomolos (or whomever) told Arcilla to get out of the car and walk up to the door.

He did because we heard the car door open and then shut. And that's the last thing we heard because the tracking function showed the phone not moving. Arcilla was moving, but he'd left the phone in the car.

"We should have told him to take the phone with him," I said.

Susannah said, "And what would you have said if he asked why? So we can eavesdrop on your conversation?"

Tristan nodded. "She's right. I should have slipped a trackable device into his clothes."

"How?" I asked.

"Just drop it into his pocket like in *The Da Vinci Code*. Maybe he'll call us after the meeting is over," Tristan suggested.

He didn't.

31

Three days later, Whit Fletcher was standing next to me at the morgue.

"Can you identify him?"

"Not by name. But I've seen him twice."

"Gimme the details."

"The first time was about two weeks ago. He came into my shop and asked if I could tell him how to get to Dos Hermanas. I gave him directions. He thanked me and left. The second time was about an hour later when I went to Dos Hermanas. He was sitting at a table by himself."

"How certain are you this is that guy? He looks like an average Joe."

"I'm totally certain because I saw him two other times."

"Why'd you tell me only two times?"

"Because the other two times I saw him were snapshots."

Then Whit remembered my camera. "So you got a picture of him coming in when he asked for directions."

"Right."

"And going out when he left."

"Right. But that one's not going to help because all it shows is the back of his head."

"The first one's not going to help either."

"Why not?"

"Because we already took a picture of his face and ran it through the facial recognition files at NCIC and got no match. And you don't know this, but when the tech transferred the picture of the woman with the pistol to the jump drive, he got the entire set of pictures from your little laptop. So of course we ran pistol woman's picture through the facial recognition files at NCIC and also got no match."

"So neither the woman with the pistol nor the guy asking for directions were in the system?"

"Right. But police work is a lot of combing through haystacks. So just to be thorough, we ran all the pictures for the last thirty days hoping we might get a match, and there was one."

"Wow. What are the odds that someone caught by my camera would be in the NCIC files?"

"Actually, the odds are not that low. There's over five hundred million faces in those files."

"And one of them visited my shop." I was still amazed. "Can he or she help you identify the dead guy?"

"I doubt it. The picture we got of him was from a camera in the security check line at Dulles airport. Security check lines are where a lot of those shots come from. Everyone who's ever boarded a plane is in the files. And the date was before either the brother or the sister was here, so it's probably just some tourist from DC who came into your shop."

"What's his name? I might remember him if he bought something."

"Fat chance."

Even though I'm used to Whit's brusque manner, I was a bit offended. "My memory is good."

"That's not what I meant. I meant fat chance he bought something."

Given that I hadn't sold anything for weeks, I probably wouldn't remember the guy. Because I deal in old valuable pots, people seeking souvenirs come in, look at the price tags under the first pots they see and quickly depart.

*   *   *

I was a bit upset at having to see another dead person for no good reason, so I said, "What I don't understand is why you asked me to ID this guy. You couldn't have known he dropped into my shop asking for directions."

"No, we didn't know that."

"Didn't the guy have any identification on him?"

"No. He had no wallet. What he did have was some loose change, an old-fashioned fountain pen, and a piece of paper torn from the *Albuquerque Journal*."

"Who walks around with no wallet?"

He smiled and said, "Probably you when you've just dug up an old pot and deliberately don't have any ID on you just in case a Bureau of Land Management law enforcement officer happens by."

"But how did you connect him with me?"

"This here piece of paper torn from the *Journal*."

He handed it to me. It was the picture of the pot Stella Ramsey had taken for her article.

I stared at the pot as the wheels of my mind spun around. The spinning didn't take me anywhere because there was no solid ground for the wheels to grab.

Whit said, "Someone called a county sheriff up north and reported the body. When the sheriff arrived and examined the body, there was no obvious cause of death. So the sheriff called the State Medical Investigator's office. They picked up the body and brought it here. A blood scan revealed a high level of sodium cyanide."

"Even I know cyanide is a poison."

"Yep. Class 1 according to the lab boys. So someone poisoned him then dropped the body off at the local church. The priest found him and called the county sheriff."

I thought for a moment then asked, "Was the priest's name Father Jerome?"

"How the hell did you know that?"

"It's a long story."

32

"Why do you always get the murder mystery stuff when you don't even like murder mysteries? And me, a true mystery fan, gets it only secondhand from you?"

"Next time Whit wants me to go to the morgue, I'll have him take you instead."

Going to the morgue probably wouldn't bother Susannah nearly as much as it bothers me. She kills animals and slices them up into chops, roasts, and steaks.

I eat those things, but I'd have to become a vegetarian if I had to do the killing and slicing.

We were back at Dos Hermanas enjoying a vegan meal of pico de gallo, house-made tostadas, and margaritas. All very delicious in spite of being vegan. I had told her all about the mystery man in the morgue.

She put her margarita on the table and said, "I remember that guy because we looked at his picture." She pointed and said, "He was at that table when we came in here later. But why would they ask you to ID him? Other than him asking for directions and sitting near us, there's no other connection between you and him is there?"

"I didn't think there was. But he had torn out the picture and article in the *Albuquerque Journal* about my little pot, and the torn paper was in his pocket."

"What!" Her eyes looked like big brown saucers. "How the . . . Wait, I got it. He didn't really come in to ask directions. He was casing the joint because he was planning to steal that little pot."

"Maybe. But his casing the joint didn't help because I still have that pot hidden away in my secret compartment."

"He . . ."

She hesitated then said, "We need to give him a name. Let's call him Arrotza."

"Arrotza? That's a name?"

"Not a name, but it fits. It means 'stranger' in Basque. He's the stranger who came into your shop, got directions to our gin mill, and then laid in wait for us at that table."

I laughed and said, "The only time anyone orders gin here is when Gladwyn orders a pink gin, so it's hardly a gin mill. And the correct phrase is *lie in wait*."

"That's the correct phrase only in two cases," she said with a mischievous look on her face.

"Okay. I'll bite. What are the two cases?"

"The first one is if he's going to fib and then wait. The second one is if you're talking to an English teacher. No real people say *lie in wait* when they mean *laid in wait*."

I held up my margarita and we clinked glasses.

"Do they know how he died?" she asked.

"Sodium cyanide. So they're treating it as a murder."

"That would be exciting, but the death might have been a suicide or an accident."

"Suicide maybe. But who accidentally ingests sodium cyanide?"

"A druggie might. Sodium cyanide is a white powder that looks like cocaine."

Susannah knows this stuff because she's read several thousand murder mysteries.

"Here's a tough question," I said. "Why did he ask me for directions to Dos Hermanas? It can't be just a coincidence that the place he wanted to find is the place I always go."

"There are no coincidences, Hubie. Maybe he came earlier when Glad was minding the store and asked where he might find you. Glad said he didn't know where you were but that it was a good bet you'd be in Dos Hermanas at five."

I nodded. "You're probably right. But here's something else puzzling. I now assume Arrotza knew I have that little pot. Anyone who reads the paper or watches television might know that. But why would he come to my shop?"

"That's the same question you asked about Arcilla. He already had a pot and you couldn't figure out why he wanted yours."

"Yeah. Turns out he thought it was a family heirloom. When he found out it was a copy he lost interest."

"Maybe it's the same for Arrotza," she said. "He thinks your pot is a family heirloom. He and Arcilla aren't on speaking terms, so Arrotza doesn't know yours is a fake because Arcilla hasn't told him."

"Maybe Nomolos told him," I replied. "Nomolos knows mine is a fake because he's the one who had Tristan make the fakes."

We sat silently for a while. I figured we were both thinking the same thing: *We have no clue.*

"I know you don't like getting crime info secondhand," I said, "but it's better than not getting it at all, right?"

"There's more?"

"Yes. And it's a bombshell. Arrotza's body was found by Father Jerome."

"Father Jerome in La Reina?"

"Yep. Someone dropped the body off in the church."

"And they don't know who the deceased is."

"They do not. He had things in his pockets like coins, a pen, and of course the torn page from the *Journal*, but he didn't have a wallet or any ID. What puzzles me is why would anyone be murdered over one of these little pots? They can be copied for about two bucks each."

"And a woman interested in the pots showed Tristan a pistol maybe accidentally on purpose," she reminded me.

"I need a logical explanation," I said.

To which she replied, "Calvin said, 'To make a bad day worse, wish for the impossible.'"

Which is what I was doing. People were trying to buy my pot and maybe steal my pot. And I had no logical explanation for that. I didn't even have an illogical explanation. The things are not valuable. Unless they have some sort of magic power or secret code like in *The Da Vinci Code* story.

33

My father-in-law-to-be dropped by the next morning and told me he wanted to talk about the wedding plans.

"Great," I said.

I gave him some orange juice because he doesn't drink coffee or any other caffeinated drinks. I also poured juice for myself because I didn't want to risk even a small dent in our newfound camaraderie by breaking one of his rules even though it is not one of mine.

He took a sip of his juice. "This tastes fresh."

"It is. I squeezed it this morning." And for the same reason I didn't offer him coffee, I did not tell him I had added a few ounces of Gruet Brut Rosé to the glass of juice I drank before he arrived.

He took a second sip, put his glass on my table, and hesitated in a way that suggested he was going to broach a delicate topic. "Would you consider having your marriage to my daughter officiated by a minister of my church?"

"I would be happy to have that happen," I replied, thinking inwardly that I'd consent to have the marriage officiated by a Rastafarian from Mr. Clarke's homeland of Jamaica if it would make him happy. Then I thought about steel drums and Bob Marley, and jerk-seasoned hors d'oeuvres served with rum punch, and the idea of a Jamaican-style wedding began to sound good.

Then I looked at the clean-shaven man across from me wearing a starched white shirt, came to my senses, and said, "My study of your religion led me to believe that your ministers are prohibited from performing marriages between someone who is a Seventh-day Adventist and someone who is not."

"That is not precisely correct," he said. "Not performing weddings between an Adventist and a non-Adventist has long been church practice. But even though it is traditional, it has never been officially voted to be policy. There was a statement in an old version of the *Minister's Manual* that said ministers should not perform the marriage ceremony of believers with unbelievers. However, the *Minister's Manual* is only a guide, not an official pronouncement of the church. A strict prohibition against ministers performing such ceremonies would have to be in the *Church Manual* which is silent on this subject. There have been discussions about adding a ban of such ceremonies to the manual, but when put to a vote, they have failed to pass. One reason is that in many areas, women members of the faith far outnumber men members. So if a woman in those areas wanted to marry she would likely have to marry a non-Adventist, and most of us believe the privilege of an Adventist minister performing the wedding ceremony should not be denied to a member simply because of demographics."

"So you would have to convince an SDA minister that there are no SDA men around here for her to marry?"

"No. That is just a reason given for it not being made policy. It is not forbidden, so the only question would be whether there is a local SDA minister who would agree to perform the ceremony."

"Have you mentioned this to Sharice?"

"Yes. She is as willing as you are." He smiled and added, "Probably for the same reason; you two would agree to almost anything to get my approval."

"Guilty as charged."

He laughed and said, "I'm not going to demand any belief changes, but I've thought more about the Sabbath matter, and I continue to believe that we *do* know which days are Sabbaths even if we have not counted every day since the universe was created. It is perfectly plausible that humans have observed the Sabbath from the very beginning and kept track even when the calendars were changed."

"I agree that is possible. Not likely in my opinion, but certainly possible. So instead of arguing from the difficulty of keeping track, let me try another approach to justify my belief that God wants us to keep every seventh day as a day of worship but doesn't care which day it is so long as we stick to that same day."

He sat back in his chair and smiled. "What is the nature of this new approach?"

"I want to try to illustrate why the exact day should not be an issue. So I start with the fact the entire earth is never in the same day. When it is, for example, Tuesday in half of the world, it is Wednesday in the other half. The dividing line is the International Date Line. Now imagine that it is Saturday on one side of the line and Sunday on the other. And that a Seventh-day Adventist is standing on the Sunday side and a Roman Catholic is standing on the Saturday side, their toes only inches from the line. Neither person is worshiping because neither is in what they consider to be the Sabbath day. Am I right?"

"So far."

"Okay. Now imagine that each of them takes one step forward. Now they are in their respective Sabbaths and can begin their worship service. Simply because they have moved twelve inches. So it seems to me that God is not a bureaucrat who quibbles over a minor detail. Stepping back and forth over an imaginary line cannot capture the true spirit of a Sabbath."

He laughed and said, "You are indeed a Pharisee. I will think about what you have said before responding. Meanwhile, there is another matter I wish to discuss. I do not approve of cohabitation. But that point now seems as silly as your date line argument. You and Sharice have conceived a child. You are soon to be married. It is clear that your love is true and strong. My presence has disrupted both her life and yours, though you have both been too kind to mention it, much less complain. So when I left you two alone in your place the other night, it was my tacit consent that you are *de facto* man and wife. If you will allow me to stay here in your living quarters, I think you and Geronimo should return to the downtown loft with Sharice and Benz."

"That is very thoughtful of you. Geronimo will not be as happy about the change as I am because he is afraid of Benz."

"So am I," said Mr. Clarke.

"There is, however, a potential problem. You know about the strange little pot I have, but I don't know how much you know about the difficulties it has caused."

"Sharice has given me the basic facts. I don't think I would be in any danger."

"Neither do I. Gladwyn tends my shop along with his own. We keep the door locked and a sign on the door informing customers that if they want to look at the merchandise, the person in the shop to the right will let them do so. The building has an alarm that would be set off if anyone attempts to enter. And the living area is separated from the shop by two locked doors."

He smiled and said, "Montreal has a relatively low crime rate for a large city, but even relatively low is a lot. There are about 750 break-ins per month. But there are almost two million residents, so the percentage is low. No one has broken into my home which, like yours, is alarmed and in a safe area. And I believe I will enjoy having Gladwyn as my temporary neighbor."

34

After Mr. Clarke left, Arcilla showed up and asked if I had any coffee brewed. I told him I didn't because my future father-in-law had been here and didn't drink coffee, and he asked if it was for health reasons.

"No. It is for religious reasons."

"He is a Mormon?"

"No. A Seventh-day Adventist. In fact, he and I were discussing the issue of which day is the real Sabbath."

"Ah. Well, the Seventh-day Adventists are right about the Sabbath but wrong about coffee."

I locked the store and we went to the back where I brewed New Mexico Piñon Coffee (dark roast), so good it's almost demonic. Maybe the SDAs are right.

Arcilla took a sip and said, "The official reasons for this visit are to return the cell phone and to thank you for arranging the meeting."

"How did it go?"

He sighed. "Not well. He is indeed the descendent of the person who left our village, and the pot he has—unlike the one you have—is a genuine family heirloom, handmade around five hundred years ago."

"So you did connect with a distant relative. That part was good, wasn't it?"

"In a historical way yes. History is more important to us than most peoples. So I can place a few pieces in the jigsaw of our family history. But—what do I call him? Perhaps cousin is close enough. Or perhaps it is more accurate to say I don't want to be any closer. He is a disagreeable person."

He let his head bow slightly and stared at the floor for a few seconds before looking up and saying, "He and his family are dysfunctional. When I asked him about the people who live in his area, he said he rarely mixes with them except when conducting business. His wife barely spoke, and when she did, she reminded me of someone from my village, and it turned out she was. It was quite a surprise. The son looks like his mother, and seems very close to both of them. But the daughter seems almost reclusive."

"So he has two children?"

"Yes, but unlike the son, the daughter doesn't look like the mother at all."

"Maybe she was adopted," I said, thinking of my own history.

He shook his head. "I don't think so. He seems quite proud of the son and somewhat distant from the daughter. I regret that this is part of our culture, favoring sons. The daughter is the older child. If he had adopted a first child, I think he would have insisted it be a male. When the son was born later, he may have paid less attention to his daughter."

Which, I thought, would explain the sister's remark that she and her brother were not on good terms, and also her having to go to my shop to try to find out what was going on in her own family.

Arcilla continued. "My view is that the family's issues stem largely from the father's profound ignorance about his ancestors and his past. I got the idea that the son has made a small bit of progress in bringing the father out of his cocoon. Perhaps he listens to the son precisely because he is a son. I tried to instruct the father, but he refused to listen. Five hundred years is a long time. His ties to the past are permanently rent."

As you know, we were conversing in Spanish. In English, *rent* almost always means what you pay for something like an apartment or a car from Hertz. But a homonym is *rent* meaning "separate into parts with force or violence," as in "the New Mexico sandstorm rent my awning into pieces."

I mention this because the Spanish verb for "to rent" as in paying for an apartment is *rentar*, and it has no homonyms.

But Spanish has two verbs that have a meaning similar to the English *rent* in the sense of "pulled apart." Those two are *desgarrar* and *rasgar*. They are basically interchangeable, but *desgarrar* is more like "to tear," and *rasgar* is more like "to rip."

Why am I giving you a Spanish grammar lesson? Because Arcilla used *rasgar* when the more appropriate word to use in that case would have been *desgarrar*.

Arcilla had said, "His ties to the past are permanently rent." But if someone loses ties to the past over time, those ties were not *ripped* because ripped implies something more sudden and violent.

Arcilla rose to his feet, shook my hand, and thanked me again for assisting him.

I walked with him to the front door, unlocked it, and said goodbye.

I sighed, re-locked the door, and started back to the living quarters. Then I decided I should leave the door unlocked while I sat at the counter and read. The shop had been closed a lot recently; maybe there was pent-up demand.

Fat chance, I thought. But I walked back to the door and unlocked it.

And saw Arcilla reach into his pocket, pull out a yarmulke, and place it on his head.

35

Susannah came by after Arcilla left, and I told her about his donning a yarmulke.

"Oh my God! He's a Jew!"

"Or he's tired of the New Mexico sun beating down on his bald spot," I joked.

Instead of laughing, she said, "I was wrong. It wasn't hair transplants. It was just a sort of semi-part caused by wearing a yarmulke."

"Exactly," I said. "When I made my list of things I knew about Arcilla, one of the items was 'Hair transplants actually work.' I added that because as he walked away from me, I noticed that the circle of visible scalp was almost completely gone. I put it down to successful transplants. But it was really just the hair going back to its normal position after not being pressed down for some time."

"You and your lists," she said with mild disdain.

I ignored that and said, "I don't understand why he never wore the yarmulke around me."

"Simple, Hubie. He didn't want you to know he's a Jew."

"He thought I'm anti-Semitic?"

"No. It doesn't have anything to do with you. He doesn't want *anyone* to know because he's a crypto-Jew."

"A secret Jew? Is that like super orthodox or something?"

"No. Crypto-Jews are people who secretly adhere to Judaism while publicly professing to be some other religion."

"Why would they do that?"

"You want the long story or the short one?"

"How about the medium story?"

"Okay. You know that Jews lost their ancestral homeland around three thousand years ago and were dispersed to many other lands. Occasionally, the rulers of those lands would decide that everyone must adhere to the religion of the rulers. So Jews were told they had to convert. In some cases the options were to convert or leave the country. In some cases, the choice was to convert or be killed."

"They wouldn't let them just leave?"

"We read about this in class, but I'm not an expert at all. I think it was in about the 12th century that one of the Muslim rulers of Spain issued a proclamation that anyone who refused to adopt Islam would be put to death and his property confiscated. Jews asked the ruler for mercy. He told them he was doing it for their own good because if they didn't accept Islam, they would suffer eternal punishment. The Jews replied that they had a different view about how their souls would be judged, and if they were wrong, it certainly wouldn't be his fault. He refused to change his mind. The Jews then proposed that he let them leave the country, but he said he would not allow his subjects to serve another king. But soon afterwards, the king, who seemed to be healthy and fit, died a sudden death. His son believed God had punished his father because of his cruelty to the Jews. The son became the ruler and said he didn't care what religion his subjects followed. But when the Muslim rulers were finally driven out by the Spaniards, it was not long until the Spanish Inquisition began. The only difference was that the Muslims wanted the Jews to become Muslims, and the Spaniards wanted the Jews to become Catholics."

I said, "I know it's difficult to understand the thought process of people who lived centuries ago, but I just don't understand why anyone would think that force can change someone's religious beliefs. I mean imagine two former Presbyterians, a woman and a man, meet in a new denomination called The Church of Gathering

Clouds, and the man asks the woman why she converted and gets the answer, 'I had a vision, and a voice spoke to me.' Then she asks the man why he converted, and he says, 'A member of The Church of Gathering Clouds threatened to kill me if I didn't.' Can she possibly take him seriously as a believer?"

"Probably not. The *conversos*, which was what the Jews who converted were called, were constantly watched and suspected of just faking being Catholics. That shows that even the inquisitors who were trying to force conversion realized the absurdity of the idea, at least subconsciously. Otherwise, why spy on the *conversos*? And *conversos* caught practicing Judaism in secret were subject to everything from wearing a *sanbenito* to being burned at the stake."

"What is a *sanbenito*?"

"It was a knee-length yellow sackcloth gown with a dunce cap for headgear, and they had to wear it at all times when they were in public."

"For how long?"

"It varied, but was often for years. So you can understand that with the options of embarrassment, death, and forced moves to a new place which might be just as hard on Jews as Spain was, some Jews decided going to the New World was the best choice because they hoped it would be easier there to maintain their religion."

"Because there was no inquisition in the Americas?"

"Actually, there was an inquisition in Mexico, but the few Spaniards in what is now New Mexico were too busy trying to subdue and convert the native peoples to worry much about whether a few of their comrades were secretly practicing Judaism."

"How do you know so much about this?"

"You won't believe this coincidence."

"You always tell me there are no coincidences."

"That's just in murder mysteries. In real life there are coincidences. And one of them is the conference I told you about."

"Where you gave a presentation on religious symbolism?"

"Right. Guess which organization sponsored the conference?"

"I have no idea."

"The Society for Crypto-Judaic Studies."

"There's actually an organization that studies that?"

"Absolutely. It all began when a guy named Stanley Hordes became New Mexico's state historian in the early 1980s. He had earned a PhD at Tulane University in New Orleans, and his dissertation dealt with the crypto-Jews of colonial Mexico. There were quite a few down there. After Hordes became the state historian, people started coming to him and telling him about crypto-Jews in New Mexico. They would tell him things like people in their village bathing on Fridays and donning clean clothes afterwards, ritually disposing of the blood drained from slaughtered animals, preferring goat meat over pork, fasting on Yom Kippur, and eating tortillas during Passover."

"Tortillas are kosher?"

"Of course. Because they are unleavened. They also told stories of people partially circumcising their sons."

I grimaced. "Partially?"

"A little slice to follow the law of Moses, but not enough to be obvious."

"Can we move to another part of the story?"

"Yeah. Let's do that so you can lose that grimace. Even though Hordes had written about the crypto-Jews of Mexico in his dissertation, he had not expected to deal with the topic in New Mexico. Evidently no one thought there were any crypto-Jews here. His main reason for taking the job in New Mexico was not an interest in crypto-Jews; it was because he likes the weather here. He grew up in the District of Columbia and did his doctoral studies in New Orleans, so he wanted to escape the humidity. He had earned his master's degree at UNM and loved the desert."

"Clearly a sensible guy," I observed. "So he came back here for the weather and then started hearing stories about crypto-Jews in New Mexico, and he had written a dissertation about crypto-Jews in Old Mexico. Another coincidence?"

She nodded. "They just keep piling up. It turns out there had been a few anti-Jewish issues here. In the late 17th century, the governor of New Mexico and his wife were accused of practicing Judaism. The same charge was made about a bureaucrat named Francisco Gómez Robledo, who was also said to have a tail, supposedly one way to identify a Jew."

"You can't be serious."

"I am. Fortunately, those three were acquitted. After that, crypto-Jews were never an issue in New Mexico so far as anyone knew."

"Until people started telling Hordes about them," I guessed.

"Right. At first Hordes thought the stories were just gossip. But as more people told him stories about the crypto-Jews in New Mexico, he began to wonder if the stories were true and that New Mexico had crypto-Jews similar to the ones in Mexico that he had described in his dissertation. He wondered if it was possible that crypto-Jews in New Mexico's isolated Hispano villages still secretly managed the feat of preserving some remnant of their forefathers' faith.

"During the time that Hordes was being dragged into the crypto-Jew story, Tomás Atencio—a professor at UNM—was also interested in the topic. Atencio remembered a time in the early 1950s when a distant relative had laughed about being able to take land from the Atencios because the relative's family were 'better Jews than all of you.' Tomás asked his father about his cousins. 'Yes,' the father said, 'there's been talk that they're Jewish.'"

"But *Atencio* is a standard Castilian name, not a Jewish name," I pointed out.

"Remember, Hubie—the cryptos were pretending to have abandoned Judaism. So they changed their names."

"They took Castilian names?"

"Some did. If they were from Spain. But remember that Jews were being pressured in Portugal and a lot of other countries. One guy at the conference was a member of an association called *Unión Sefardí Mundial*. Did I pronounce that right?"

"Almost like a native."

She smiled. "In his presentation, he listed twelve family names that are common among people in Spanish-speaking countries that likely have Sephardic origins. I don't remember all twelve, but I remember a few that are common here: Castro, Espinoza, and Medina. But some of them didn't want to take a surname used by Spaniards, so they took common nouns as their names."

"Such as?"

"*Rueda*."

"Why would someone take *wheel* as a family name?"

"Because they couldn't use a Hebrew name and didn't want a Christian one."

I thought about it briefly. "So I'm guessing Cabrera, Carvalho, and Silva might also be surnames used by crypto-Jews."

"Why?"

"Because they're common nouns: *cabrera* means 'goat herder,' *carvalho* means 'oak,' and *silva* means 'forest.'"

"There are a lot of New Mexicans with those names," she said. "The guy from *Unión Sefardí Mundial* said that because of changing demographics over the centuries, people with names that used to be associated with Sephardic heritage are not all that likely to have Sephardic roots."

I told her I had another name to add to the list. "It's one of my favorite obscure thinkers. And you can probably guess which one."

"Spinoza."

"Right. I'm impressed."

"You shouldn't be. The only other ones I can think of are Pythagoras and Ptolemy, and it's a safe bet they weren't Jews, Sephardic or otherwise. What does Spinoza mean?"

"*Thorny*. It's his name and also a description of his philosophy. But let's get back to the topic at hand. Besides this Hordes guy and the professor at UNM, who else was uncovering evidence of crypto-Jews in New Mexico?"

"Emilio and Trudi Coca, an elderly couple who lived in New Mexico, told Hordes they had visited Hispano graveyards where they found and photographed headstones inscribed with surprising first names, *Adonay* for example, the Hebrew word for Lord. They also had pictures of graves with the Star of David on them."

I shook my head. "I thought I knew almost everything about my state, but I've never heard of this."

"It gets even better. Hordes resigned his state job in 1985 and began spending more and more time promoting his growing belief that Sephardic crypto-Judaism had survived centuries of secrecy in New Mexico. His theory had enormous appeal for Jews everywhere, for whom the Holocaust was still fresh in their minds and who longed for positive stories about Jewish survival. In 1987, National Public Radio broadcast an interview in which Hordes explained his theory about the crypto-Jews of New Mexico. Many people bought tapes of that interview. Stories about the crypto-Jews suddenly appeared in US and international news outlets. Hordes had his fifteen minutes of fame. He was interviewed by the *New York Times*, CNN, and the *Jerusalem Post*."

"Wow. The *Jerusalem Post*?"

She nodded.

I said, "I just thought of something. When I asked Arcilla how his meeting went with Nomolos, he said Nomolos and his family are dysfunctional. He said Nomolos misunderstands some very important matters about both his past and his beliefs. And here is the part that now seems even more significant to me: He said, 'I tried to instruct him but he refused to listen. Five hundred years is a long time. His ties to the past are permanently rent.'"

"So?"

"We were conversing in Spanish which has two verbs for *torn*. The one he used is the one that would describe the Jewish tradition of tearing your clothes as a sign of grief at a funeral."

She nodded. "So you're saying that Arcilla basically considers Nomolos to be dead. Not physically, but in some other way."

"Exactly. He considers Nomolos to be spiritually dead, maybe because Nomolos has stopped being a crypto-Jew."

She shook her head. "No. More likely because being a crypto-Jew five hundred years ago was simply being a Jew who kept his practice of Judaism secret. But after five hundred years and being cut off from other Jews and having no synagogues or rabbis, some of the so-called crypto-Jews are not practicing Judaism. They are simply following some rules and practices passed down by their forbearers with little or no understanding of where those practices came from and what they mean."

I figured she was right, in part because of her studies of religious symbolism, but mostly because what she said made sense.

"You and I know someone who might know more about the crypto-Jews in the Hispano villages," I said.

She smiled. "Father Jerome."

36

The first time we went to La Reina, I remembered thinking the trip took us five-thousand feet up in elevation and five hundred years back in time.

The road we had watched the icon of Arcilla's car (which I now figured was a rental) traverse was a primitive trail that snaked along a creek and eventually up to the spring that fed the stream. My old Bronco bumped and swayed but followed the road like a horse who'd been down it before. Which it had.

La Reina is a village time has forgotten, and the villagers seem to like it that way. Low adobes are scattered around a system of *acequias* that allow water to flow to plots of corn, beans, chiles, and small orchards of apples and apricots. The road—if you can call it that—leads to a hard-packed dirt *placita* surrounded by a general store, a gas station, a town hall, a hair salon, a grocery store, one empty store, a church, and a café and bar named *El Eructo del Rey*, which means "The King's Belch" in English. There's probably a story behind that name, but I don't think I want to know it.

The last time we'd been here, there were two empty stores. One of them was now a feed store.

We found Father Jerome (a.k.a Álvar Nuñez) in the church.

Hardly a surprise. What was a surprise was that *La Viuda de Cheche Zaragosa Medrano* (the widow of Cheche Zaragosa

Medrano) was sitting next to him in one of the pews. We had called ahead, told him what we wanted, and he had taken the liberty of inviting her to join us.

She is the village *curandera*, which means she's a folk healer, medicine woman, herbalist, spiritualist, shaman, or some combination of all or most of those.

The Widow Zaragosa does not speak English. She smiled at Susannah and said, "*Buenos dias, bruja.*" (Good morning, witch).

The confusion that led *La Curandera* to think Susannah was a witch began when Susannah asked me the Spanish word for *ice*. I thought she said *eyes* because she was flirting with Baltazar, the bartender who had great eyes, and I thought she wanted to tell him that. So I told her the word is *ojos*, and she ordered *Pepsi con ojos*—Pepsi with eyes.

I had cleared that up with the Widow Zaragosa, and it was good to see that she could now joke about it.

She also said proudly that the village had changed dramatically since our last visit. One of the empty stores was now a feed store, and two children had been born.

I managed to keep a straight face and tell her it was good that the village was prospering.

I asked Father Jerome about finding the body in the church.

He crossed himself and said, "A shock obviously. I came in that morning around 9:00 and saw him on the floor. I thought at first that he was asleep. Nights can be cold up here even in early June, and sometimes people who've had too many drinks at *El Eructo del Rey* decide to sleep it off in the church rather than walk a mile or two up the mountain to their houses."

"The church is open late at night?"

"The church is always open; there is no lock on the door. When I tried to wake him by shaking his arm, I realized his arm was cold. Very cold. He had been dead long enough that his body temperature had dropped significantly. I administered last rites. Then I called the sheriff."

"Did you recognize the man?"

"No."

"I assumed you knew everyone in town."

"I do. And many of the people in the county. But there are a few families who live up in the mountains or just don't mix much."

"Do you know anyone named Nomolos?"

"No. In fact, even though it sounds like an Hispanic name, I've never heard of it."

Susannah asked him if he knew of any crypto-Jews in the area. He thought about it for a minute or so. "I have heard stories. But nothing that has convinced me there are any Jews in the county, crypto or otherwise."

"Please indulge my curiosity. Can you give any specifics about the stories you heard?"

"They were told to me in confidence."

"In the confessional?"

"No. But in ordinary confidence."

"I don't know whether anyone has told you yet, but the State Medical Examiner thinks the man whose body you discovered was murdered."

He nodded. "The local sheriff told me that after he learned of it."

"We have reason to think the victim was a crypto-Jew. The stories you've been told might help us discover who he was and maybe even who killed him."

"Perhaps it would be more appropriate for me to discuss it with a law enforcement official."

I could see Susannah deflate. But she took it as stoically as possible. "It's good to see you again," she said, and stood up and stepped into the aisle.

"¡Espere!" said the Widow Zaragosa.

I had been translating for her, but she had sat silently while we talked. Now she was ordering Susannah to wait. She looked at Father Jerome and reminded him that Susannah was the one who had persisted in believing that the body I found in that cliff dwelling was a modern-day person, not a mummy. And that he had been murdered. And that thanks to Susannah, his family had been able to give him a proper Christian burial. And that Susannah had even returned for the services for Carlos Campos Castillo even though she did not know him or his family.

The priest asked Susannah to sit down. He said to her, "I do not give credence to these tales, but you may have more insight than do I. The first one is that there was a family with a dreidel."

Susannah laughed and said, "I wouldn't give that any credence myself. Dreidels are part of the Ashkenazi culture. They are not used by or even generally known of by Sephardic Jews. What some Sephardic Jews do have is the *trompita,* a wooden top Hispanic kids play with regardless of their religion."

"I am impressed," said the good father, smiling broadly. "How did you come to have such detailed knowledge of both major branches of Judaism? I know you are Catholic because I heard your confession."

"I'm an art historian, and my main specialty is religious symbolism in paintings."

"She teaches art history at the University of New Mexico," I said proudly. I left out the adjunct part.

"What other stories have you been told?" Susannah asked.

"That a certain family lights a candle every Friday night."

"I don't suppose they added information about other nights?"

He smiled. "My thought as well. I light a candle every night, and I can assure you I am not a Jew, crypto or otherwise."

"Other stories?"

"Draining the blood from slaughtered animals," he said. "I was raised in Hatch. Everyone I knew drained the blood from chickens. None of those people were Jews. They just had the good sense not to want to eat chicken blood."

It looked like nothing he had heard would relate to or help us with the pot matter. But just to make sure, I took my little pot out of my pocket and showed it to him.

I could see the surprise in his eyes. "I have seen this pot. Or one very similar to it. There is a gold mining operation not far from here. I was seeking donations to make repairs to the church. These old adobe buildings require a good deal of maintenance. Several parishioners work now and again for the mine, and they said the company makes a lot of money."

He hesitated a moment and smiled. Then he said, "I saw my asking for a donation as serving two purposes at once. The first was that we needed the money. The second was it would be an opportunity for the mine owner to do penitence."

"Penitence for what?"

"Three things. First, he took advantage of his unskilled workers by running a ten-for-twelve scam."

"What's a ten-for-twelve scam?"

"The workers were paid hourly and were mostly part-time, so at the end of the week, they often didn't have enough money to get by until the next payday. The owner told them they could borrow ten dollars from him on any Friday, but they had to pay back twelve dollars the next Friday."

I was stunned. "That's an annual percentage rate of one thousand and forty percent!"

The priest shrugged. "The workers are unlikely to know about loan interest or percentages. They take the ten dollars, spend it over the weekend, and then repeat the process the next week. Often they are forced to do unpaid overtime to get back to even."

"That's disgusting," said Susannah. "Is it even legal?"

"I don't know. But who's going to take legal action on a ten-dollar handshake loan with no paperwork?"

"What were the other things he had to atone for?" I asked.

"The second one is that when he extended his mining operation, he destroyed an Anasazi site."

I said, "But you can't get a mining permit until you have an archaeological survey to make sure there are no such sites where you plan to dig."

Given what I do, I felt a bit hypocritical for pointing it out. But I don't destroy sites. I treat them with reverence and rescue their pots as their makers desire.

"He had such a survey made," Father Jerome said, "but the archaeologist who made the survey certified that there were no cultural assets."

"Do you remember the archaeologist's name?"

"Yes. Bruno Biegler."

My surprise must have shown on my face because Father Jerome asked, "You know of him?"

"I do. He is anathema in the archaeological community."

The priest nodded. "It is widely believed in this community that he took a bribe to make a clean report."

"And the third thing the mine owner had to atone for?"

"It would be inappropriate for me to say because there is no proof of his other alleged misdeed."

"Do you know him?"

"I have never met him. When I went to the mining company, the only person I saw was a young woman in the office. Behind her was a window into a workshop where I saw shelves and cabinets, various tools, and a work table with a vice, a bench-mounted grinder, and other implements. The little pot was on the workbench. Pottery is everywhere in New Mexico. I noticed that little pot only because it was so different. I'm not particularly adept at fundraising, so I tried to break the ice by asking her about the pot. She said it was something she'd rather not talk about, which made me feel even less adept. So I asked her if I could speak to someone in charge. She said, 'So you assume I'm not in charge because I'm a woman?' Then, feeling like a bumbler, I gave a brief summary of what the church needs and why and asked if the company might be willing to donate. She said the owner was—in her words—'a crazy old bastard,' and that he did not make charitable donations."

"What is the name of the company?"

He laughed. "Solomon's Mines."

"Like in the Bible?" I asked.

"Yes. Of course the legend of Solomon and his gold have been enhanced in contemporary times by a book and a couple of films."

"Is the owner actually named Solomon?"

"I doubt it. I assume the name was based on the tales of Solomon's mines in the Old Testament."

37

We got directions to Solomon's Mines from Father Jerome. And laughed each time one of us said *Solomon's Mines*. It's such a cliché.

But in this case it was real. We backtracked on the dirt road but not all the way back to Ojo Caliente, just to the village of La Madera.

Susannah used her phone to find the Wikipedia page for La Madera and was surprised to find there is one.

She read it to me as we left the village headed north on State Road 519. "La Madera is a community located in the mountains of northern New Mexico and nestled within the confines of the Kit Carson National Forest. The village is surrounded by many Hispano communities."

I let the word *Hispano* trot around in my head looking for a connection. Whether it found one I wasn't certain.

We turned onto a National Forest Road which, although not paved, had a wide and smooth gravel surface which we appreciated when we met a logging truck and later a large Mack truck mounded with crushed rock which I assumed was ore of some sort. More than $40 million worth of minerals have come from Rio Arriba County since mining began of the significant deposits of copper, silver, gold, pumice, and rare-earth elements.

I have no idea what rare-earth elements are, but Tristan told me they are used in high tech stuff like lasers.

Solomon's Mines had a wide paved driveway that ran about fifty feet east from the road and then forked with the left part curving around to the back of a building which was a two-story metal structure, and the right part leading to the front that was a wooden single-story building with a small parking area that held two cars and three pickups. I assumed the large metal building was where they processed some of the ores, and the small wooden one was the business office.

Susannah stayed outside, acting as if she were taking pictures of the scenery.

I went inside. The young woman who had a pistol in her purse when she went to Spirits in Clay was behind the counter. I glanced away quickly to hide my surprise and noticed the workshop Father Jerome had told us about. No pot of any sort was on the workbench. I guessed it had been moved to prevent breakage because the current project on the bench involved putting some pieces of metal together, and pottery doesn't mix well with metalworking. There was a round metal base with an upright section, and two horizontal arms that slanted down slightly. I knew the project was unfinished because there were a bunch of smaller pieces still on the table. Except for the setting, I might have guessed it was something from IKEA and the person was taking a break trying to figure out the assembly directions.

Remembering the faux pas of Father Jerome, I said to the young lady, "You must be the person in charge."

She frowned and replied, "Why do you say that?"

"Because I assume the workers are in the big part of the building at the back or out on a job. So that leaves you as the boss."

"I suppose I am in charge, but only because everyone else is gone. We are closed today."

I smiled and said, "Sorry. Had I known that, I would not have bothered you. But the door was open, so I assumed—"

"Not many people come around here, so I don't bother to lock the door. I'll lock it after you leave," she said and started to the door jangling a key ring.

"I'd like to ask one question before I go," I said as I trailed behind her. "I know you probably get tired of this, but is your name really Solomon or is that just a clever name for a mining company?"

She laughed. "My name is Lauri B."

"Why the B?"

"The local game warden has a daughter named Lauri. She's my best friend. She goes by Lauri A because her middle name is Alice."

"I'll bet your middle name is Betsy."

"Nope."

"Beatrice?"

She smiled. "You'll never guess in a million years."

"Sure I will. There are only so many feminine names."

"It's not a feminine name."

"It's a boy's name?"

"No. It's a last name given to me as a middle name."

"You're right. I'll never guess."

We had reached the front door. I was looking through the glass out to the parking lot, but paying more attention to the glass.

I opened the door and stepped outside. "Nice to meet you, Lauri B," I said.

She caught the door before it closed and said, "The B stands for Biegler."

Then she locked the door and headed back to the office.

Biegler is not a common name, especially in New Mexico. It seemed obvious her middle name was a show of appreciation for the archaeologist who overlooked the existence of an ancient site in order for the Solomon Mining Company to get a license to mine in an expanded area.

Susannah and I got back in the Bronco.

"You get her picture?" I asked.

"Of course. With the telephoto lens in my phone, it looks like I was standing across the counter from her."

"Turns out taking those pictures was unnecessary. We already have a picture of her."

"Huh?"

"She's the woman with the pistol in her purse that Tristan saw in my shop."

"Wow! We're on the right trail. You learn anything talking to her?"

"Yes. Her middle name is Biegler."

"Isn't that the name of the archaeologist Father Jerome mentioned and you know?"

"Yes. But I don't know him. I just know about him."

"But her having the guy's middle name is significant, right?"

"Right. But not as significant as what I saw on my way out."

"Which is?"

"The big sign on the front window."

She frowned. "It says Solomon's Mines. What's significant about that?"

"I read it coming out.

"So?"

"Look at the window and pretend you're standing behind it inside the office. Then read it left to right letter by letter including spaces and punctuation."

She said, "*s, e, n, i, m,* space, then *s,* apostrophe, *n, o, m, o, l, o, s*—Oh my God! Nomolos is Solomon backwards!"

38

As we were driving back to Albuquerque, I had Susannah call Tristan and ask him to meet us at Spirits in Clay.

He went there early and actually sold a pot to a tourist. It was a small recently-made one from Acoma, not an illegally unearthed Anasazi, so it was priced at only $200. But it was the first revenue in weeks, and I decided to take it as an omen.

I told Tristan I had seen pistol girl at Solomon's Mines.

Susannah added, "We suspect her last name might be Solomon."

"Why do you suspect that?"

"Because it's the name of the company where she works: Solomon's Mines."

"Like in the Bible."

"Right. And Solomon is Nomolos spelled backwards."

"Unbelievable. No wonder we never heard that name. It isn't one. Why did she want information about your little pot?"

I shrugged. "I have no idea. Before I could ask, she told me they were closed and headed for the door to lock it behind me."

"So she was totally uncooperative?"

I shook my head. "Actually, she was sort of friendly. She told me her name is Lauri B."

"Giving you only the first letter of her surname is not totally cooperative."

"B is not the first letter of her surname; it's the first letter of her middle name which is Biegler."

"Odd middle name."

"Yes. It's the last name of a disreputable archaeologist who is thought to have falsified an archaeological survey that gave the Solomon Mining Company permission to dig in a new area. I think we need to call Whit."

Tristan and Susannah both reached for their cell phones. My land line was on the ledge under the counter, but I didn't even think about it.

When Whit arrived, I told him about our trip north.

He looked at Susannah and smiled. "So you took surreptitious photos of someone who may be a suspect in a felony. You're gonna get hauled in one of these days for impersonating an officer. But it won't be by me. I take help from anywhere I can get it." He looked at the picture on Susannah's phone. "Yep. That's pistol girl, alright."

"You shouldn't call her a girl," Susannah chided him teasingly, "She's a woman."

"When you're my age, any female under thirty is a girl, and any male under thirty is a boy."

Then he looked at me and said, "You remember that match we got from NCIC for one of the pictures on your security camera."

"The guy boarding a plane at Dulles."

"Right. We now have his name. It took a few days because he'd never been in the system before. So they had to go through the passenger manifestos to put a name with the face. His name is—"

"Solomon," I said.

He stared at me. "No. His name is Alazar Minero. Why did you guess Solomon?"

"Because when I showed Father Jerome the little pot, he said he had seen one just like it at a place called Solomon's Mines."

He laughed. "And you thought the family who runs it is named Solomon? Everyone knows about that company, mostly thanks to the name because everyone knows about King Solomon's mines in the Old Testament. They must've chosen that name just to promote the business. Like Captain Morgan Rum, which came out three hunnerd years after the Captain was dead, but people heard of him and it helped sell the stuff."

"You seem to know a lot about it."

"So I have a little rum and coke at night."

Then for no reason I can think of except for Whit being in law enforcement, I asked him if he'd ever heard of a ten-for-twelve scam.

"You musta heard about it on your trip up north because ole Triple T up there told me the Solomon's Mine guy is notorious for it."

"Who is old Triple T?"

"The sheriff. His real name is Teodoro Todero, and his nickname is *Tio*—Uncle—because he's related to half the people up there, which is why no one ever runs against him when he's up for reelection. So he's Tio Teodoro Todero, and everybody just shortens it to Triple T."

"I can see why," said Susannah.

I said, "The ten-for-twelve thing sounds like a form of usury. Jews—fairly or unfairly—have for centuries been associated with usury."

Susannah said, "Mostly unfairly. Jews were prohibited by the Law of Moses to take interest from other Jews. But after the diaspora, many of them ended up living in countries that limited what they could do. They often could not own land or enter certain professions. Some of them became bankers and of course charged interest to make a living. That doesn't make them usurers."

Whit said, "I don't know anything about his religion, but some of the uranium miners in New Mexico did the same thing, and they weren't Jews." Then he laughed and said, "Guess what Triple T calls that mine owner?"

"Solomon?"

"No."

"Loan shark?"

"No."

"I give up."

"Arnold Schwarzenegger."

"Why?"

"Because he has a housekeeper who looks exactly like his son."

Susannah said, "That's the other thing he had to do penitence for!"

Whit blurted out, "He admitted fathering the boy with his housekeeper?"

"No. But Father Jerome said the guy had three things he needed to do penitence for. The first was the ten-for-twelve scam. The second was bribing an archaeologist to overlook an Anasazi site where the mine owner wanted to dig. The third one he didn't want to tell us about, but that must be it."

Whit said, "Probably told the priest about it in the confessional, so of course the priest can't tell anyone."

"I don't think the mine owner makes confessions. I think he's a Jew."

Whit said, "Oh, so that's why you threw in that part about usury. But I doubt that the mine owner is a real Jew. If anything, he's probably a crypto-Jew."

"You know about crypto-Jews?" I asked. I hate to admit it, but I disliked learning that Whit knew an interesting factoid about New Mexico that I had just recently learned of.

"'Course I know about them. Learned about 'em in a training session."

"Why would you have a training session on crypto-Jews?"

"It wasn't just crypto-Jews. It also covered Sufis, Sunni Muslims, Shiite Muslims, Buddhists, Hindus, and Mormons."

I shook my head, blinked, then said, "Why?"

"So's we'd be sensitive to their beliefs. There's been no training session on Jews, Protestants, or Catholics. I guess because they're too ordinary."

"You deal much with the ones that aren't ordinary?"

"Nope. They must be law-abiding. How about we fire up your computer, Hubert, and look at all the mugs who might be connected with that little pot you have and may not be so law-abiding?"

The breakthrough came when Tristan saw Arrotza (as Susannah had named him) and almost shouted, "That's the guy who brought the pot, the 3-D printer, the clay and all the other stuff for me to make copies!"

"Better known to me," said Whit, "as the stiff we're still trying to ID."

I looked at him and said, "I think his last name is Minero."

"Why?" asked Whit.

"Because he is related to the Minero who you identified via NCIC."

"Explain it for me."

I had to arrange my thoughts. When I'd done so, I said, "A guy calling himself Nomolos called UNM because he wanted to find someone to set up a 3-D printer to make copies of a pot he owned. UNM sent the request to the two departments most likely to be involved with 3-D printing—computer science and art. Tristan ended up getting the job. Nomolos—let's call him that for now—told Tristan over the phone that he was sending someone to deliver the printer, the pot to be copied, some clay, some sandpaper, and some cash. But the guy who came was actually Nomolos himself."

"Then why did he tell me he was sending someone?" asked Tristan.

"Because he wanted to remain incognito. That's also why he paid in cash instead of with a check or by card. And why he used an alias."

"Why use *Nomolos* as an alias?"

"My guess is he was walking out of his office, looked at the sign that has *Solomon* on it and realized—like I did—that *Nomolos* is *Solomon* spelled backwards, which *could* be a name and would also be easy for him to remember. If he used a normal name like 'Gomez' he might later slip up and call himself 'Gonzalez.'"

"That happens all the time in murder mysteries," Susannah said. "Picking an alias is important."

Whit just stared at her and shook his head.

Then Susannah asked, "But why didn't Tristan recognize him when we were all here looking at the pictures on your camera? The first picture of course was all of us coming in from Dos Hermanas. Then directions guy leaving, then directions guy coming in and so on."

"Directions guy was Nomolos," I said. "And if Tristan had seen that picture, he would have recognized him. Not as directions guy, not as Nomolos, but as the guy Nomolos sent over. But there was no one sent over. Nomolos brought the stuff himself. Tristan didn't see those first pictures because he had taken his book bag back to the living quarters to store it away. When he got back, we were looking at the guy we called Arcilla."

"And making fun of your hair," Tristan said. Then he added, "You're right. This is the first time I've seen that picture. It's definitely the guy who brought the stuff."

Whit shook his head, then pushed his silver hair off his forehead and said, "I need you to write down all the characters' names in this here little square dance and what you know about 'em."

"Okay. But first let me show you one more picture." I scrolled down—or maybe up—I've sort of lost track of which pictures we saw in which order. But I found the one I wanted and said, "This guy is probably also named Minero. He's the son of the dead guy and the brother of pistol girl. And the guy we've been calling Arcilla is a distant relative of all of them."

Whit plopped down in a chair and said, "Somebody get me an aspirin."

After Whit swallowed the aspirin, he took the list I'd just written up for him and left.

39

I was happy Whit left because I wanted to discuss the pot thing with Susannah and Tristan without a cop listening in.

I told them I had believed all along that Arcilla—now known to us as Señor Alazar Minero—was a resident of one of New Mexico's Hispano villages. But I had now come to believe I was wrong about that.

Susannah said, "Sounds like you're going to explain that to us."

"I am."

"How long will it take?"

"With your input and questions, probably an hour or so."

"What I figured," she said. "I'd normally suggest we go to Dos Hermanas, but this conversation is probably one you don't want overheard. It is way past 5:00, so how about I mix some margaritas in that contraption Tristan gave you?"

"Think you can handle it?"

"Can't be tougher than operating a backhoe."

Tristan laughed and said he'd be her assistant, and in less than five minutes we had our drinks and were seated around my table.

"I'll start with the second time Arcilla came to my shop," I began. "He was more relaxed—or maybe *resigned* is the word. He said the story of the pots was long and complicated. I asked him if it would go well with coffee. I locked the shop and we went to the living area where I brewed some coffee. After he tasted it, he said 'I did not think it would be possible to taste such excellent coffee here.'"

I paused.

Susannah asked, "That's significant?"

"I think so. You can be the judge when you have the entire picture. The next thing he said was that his family has lived in the same village in the north on property granted to them by the king in the 17th century. Then he said that many generations ago, a member of the family decided to seek a new life. He was the youngest of five sons and realized his legacy would be small. Then Arcilla said about the family member who decided to seek a new life, 'there was another reason I will not speak of.'"

"And I suppose he didn't speak about it?"

"He did not, but I'll come back to it. He did go on to say that the family member was determined to travel to the Far West. And that in those days, a family member who moved away was usually never seen again, and some families held a wake—without a body of course—because like death, a move to far away usually meant never seeing the person again."

"Is that everything he said?"

"It's everything that deals with my false analysis."

"So lay it out for us, Sherlock!"

"This is fun," said Tristan.

"Okay, I'll try to do it by the numbers: Number one: the good coffee. 'I did not think it would be possible to taste such excellent coffee here' is something someone from Seattle might say, but not what a guy from a place like La Reina would say. There are no Starbucks in Hispano villages. They boil coffee in old tin pots. If he were from one of those places, he could not have been surprised that my coffee was better than he expected."

Susannah shook her head. "Sounds a bit weak."

"It's just one point. Each one adds up. Next is Number two: his family has lived in the same village in the north on property granted to them by the King in the 17th century."

"Did that turn out not to be the case?" she asked.

"No. But it turned out not to support my theory about where he was from. So on to Number three: the family member who wanted to seek a new life had, according to Arcilla, 'another reason I will not speak of.' As I said, he did not speak of it, but I now know what that reason was."

She started to say something, but I held up my hand and continued. "He also said that the family member who moved away was determined to go to the Far West. I assumed that meant the family member had gone to California. Remember that for the most part, North America was settled from east to west. Greeley hadn't yet advised young men to go west because he hadn't been born. I don't remember when the Spaniards started building all those missions in California, but it was later than New Mexico, and maybe the family member with wanderlust headed out there."

"So that's everything?" she asked.

"It's all of the background that I reasoned about incorrectly. Here the correct conclusion: Arcilla—Minero—is from Spain."

Tristan said, "I don't see how those things prove he's from Spain."

"Neither did I. I thought they proved he was from northern New Mexico because his village is in the north where New Mexico land grants were given by the King of Spain in the 17th century. But Spain has villages in the north, and the king also gave land grants there, not just in the new world. And they have great coffee in Spain, so Arcilla was surprised that he found good coffee in New Mexico."

"That just shows those things are *compatible* with him being from Spain," Susannah said. "It doesn't *prove* he's from Spain."

"I'll grant that. But here are the other things that point to Spain. First, his accent."

"We talked that one to death and got nowhere," she said.

I turned to Tristan and told him to use his phone to go to a site where we could hear a Galician speaking Spanish.

He didn't hesitate because he believes there is nothing you cannot read, see, or hear on the internet.

"How do you spell Galician?" he asked.

I told him, and in less than two minutes we were hearing someone who sounded like Arcilla. And I suppose one auditory stimulus led to another because Tristan said, "Remember when I said the voice of the guy talking to Arcilla as he drove north sounded familiar to me? Now I know who it was. It was the guy who brought the stuff to me. Who we now know was Nomolos."

Susannah looked at Tristan and said, "I told you that paying attention to the sounds instead of the words would help."

Then she looked at me and said, "But how did you figure out that Arcilla was Galician?"

"I looked at a map of Spain. The northernmost province is Galicia. Then I read about Galicia in my encyclopedia where I learned that they speak a language which, like Portuguese, is related to Castilian Spanish but not identical. Most people who speak Galician also speak Castilian, but with an accent."

I don't have internet, but it is still possible to learn a lot from books.

"After that," I said, "a bunch of other things started to fit into the puzzle."

"Such as?"

"Whit said the photo of Arcilla in the NCIC was from the camera in the security check line in Dulles airport. A lot of flights from Spain land there."

"I'll bet there's more," said Tristan, smiling.

"Right. Arcilla said he speaks three languages, but he wouldn't tell me what they are."

"Except that one of them was *not* English," Susannah said and we all laughed.

"Right. The two other than Spanish are Galician and . . ."

I waited while they thought. When they didn't come up with an answer, I gave them a clue by turning around and pointing to my newly-discovered bald spot.

"Hebrew!" They shouted in unison.

"Right. Which leads back to my point three: The family member who wanted to seek a new life had, according to Arcilla, 'another reason I will not speak of.'"

They both stared at me.

I said nothing. I could see their wheels turning.

"He was escaping the Inquisition!" said Susannah, and Tristan nodded.

"Exactly. Want to hear another boneheaded mistake in reasoning I made?"

"Sure," they both said, a little too enthusiastically in my view.

I looked at Susannah. "I bought your explanation that the reason Arcilla never wore his yarmulke around me was that he was a crypto-Jew. But if he were a crypto-Jew, he wouldn't have put it on in broad daylight in Old Town."

"Is there still more?" asked Tristan. He was loving the parade of errors by his uncle.

"Yes. When I told him how thin the walls of the copied pot were compared to the old handmade one he has, he asked me what three eighths of an inch is in millimeters. Only a European would ask that."

"More?" asked Susannah.

"When I asked if I could call him, he said, 'At home, yes. But not while I am travelling.' Then he handed me a piece of paper and said, 'Here is my number if you ever need to call me when I am back home.' I stuck the paper in my pocket."

"And?" she said.

"I never looked at it because he was never home so the number was useless. Then later when I started doubting my belief that he was a Hispano from New Mexico, I looked at the paper."

I gave Susannah the paper.

She stared at the number for a while. I supposed she was trying to see if it meant anything to her. Then she read it out loud: "34 276 578 0332. I'm guessing 34 is the country code for Spain."

I nodded then said, "There's more. Arcilla said to me 'History is more important to us than most peoples.' That sounds like something a Jew would be more likely to say than a crypto-Jew."

"Crypto-Jews try to keep their traditions alive," Susannah said.

"Right. But having no rabbis and no synagogues to attend makes it difficult. So the father in a crypto-Jewish family four or five centuries ago tells his children about the traditions of Chanukah, Rosh Hashanah, Passover, etc. But they don't write it down because they are illiterate and/or don't want it written down. The children try to pass along the traditions by explaining it to their children. Think how much of it is either lost or altered after a dozen generations."

"It's like that party game," said Tristan, "where everyone sits in a circle. The first person whispers a written sentence to the second person who whispers it to the third person, and so on. When it gets to the last person, she says it out loud. The original sentence is then read out loud, and everyone realizes how different the two are."

"Exactly," I said. "For example, I would guess that some of the crypto-Jews who eat tortillas during Passover have never heard the word *unleavened*."

"What else?" Tristan asked.

"When I told Arcilla that Sharice's father avoids coffee for religious reasons, he asked me if her father was a Mormon. I told him he was a Seventh-day Adventist, to which he replied, "Well, the Seventh-day Adventists are right about the Sabbath but wrong about coffee."

"More?" asked Tristan.

"No."

Susannah said, "We need to—"

And that's as far as she got because I said, "Oh my God! I just remembered something else Arcilla told me. He said when the wife spoke, she sounded like someone from his village."

Tristan said, incredulously, "A guy from a rural village in northern New Mexico married a woman from Galicia?"

"Doesn't sound likely," I admitted.

"Wait!" said Susannah. "Remember Whit told us the sheriff up there calls the mine owner Arnold Schwarzenegger because he fathered a child with the housekeeper? The woman Arcilla talked to and assumed was the wife must have actually been the housekeeper."

"How is having a housekeeper from Galicia more likely than having a wife from Galicia?"

The three of us sat in silence for a couple of minutes. Then Susannah said, "I think I've got it. Nomolos married a woman from New Mexico. The daughter is their child because she is the oldest. Which is consistent with her middle name being Biegler. She was here when they extended their mining operation. The woman from Galicia wasn't on the scene. When the wife didn't get pregnant again, Nomolos got another woman because he wanted a son as Whit told us."

"Define *got*," Tristan said.

"I'll come back to that. Nomolos and the new woman have a son. The son looks like the mother, so when Arcilla was with what he took to be the family, the four people he was actually seeing were Nomolos, the woman from Galicia, the son who looks like her because she is in fact his mother, and the daughter who doesn't look like her because she is not her daughter. She's the daughter of the first woman—the one from New Mexico who we assume Nomolos is married to. Arcilla naturally assumed the woman he saw is the wife, and both children are hers even though the daughter doesn't look like her. And the real wife was not there because . . . well, you can come up with lots of good reasons; she was ashamed, angry, locked in a closet, or whatever."

"And the *got* part?" Tristan asked again. "I buy the part about Nomolos wanting a son and neededing another woman to produce one. And given what we know about his character, he's probably not above taking a mistress to get a son. But from Galicia?"

The three of us sat there thinking. I took a sip of my margarita. It didn't help me figure out how a guy from northern New Mexico could get a mistress from Galicia, but it did taste good.

It was Susannah who finally spoke. "Likely fact: Nomolos wanted a woman to give him a son. Hypothesis one: He wanted the woman to be a Jew. Remember that Jewishness is transmitted through the mother. A child born to a Jewish man and a gentile woman is not considered a Jew. Hypothesis two: He wanted a Sephardic Jew because that's what he is. Or was before a lot of it got lost over the generations. But he still knows his family was from Galicia. So, let's try Hubie's phone trick again." She looked at Tristan and said, "See if there's a Sephardic and/or Galician dating service."

I said, "You think Nomolos had internet access?"

Susannah said, "He may have been weird and a 'crazy old bastard' as his daughter described him, but he ran a successful mining operation. You can't do that these days without the internet."

"You're right," said Tristan as he pulled out his phone and started punching buttons. "Yep. Here's the website for Solomon's Mines."

Then Tristan started punching the screen again. After a few

minutes, he looked up with a bit of surprise on his face. "There's a bunch of Sephardic dating sites. Who knew? Here's one called loveawake.com. It says, 'Welcome to Spanish Jewish free online dating site helping to connect lonely hearts around the world.' He could have found her online."

"Okay," said Susannah, "I can buy that. If I'm a lonely Spanish Jew in Spain, and I see a guy online who lives in an exotic location in the States and owns a gold mine, I might start a chat with him. And if the chat turned into an ongoing conversation that both of us enjoy, I might agree to fly to New Mexico and meet him. But it would be a short stay if I discovered he was married."

"The key," said Tristan, "is the *if*. But he's not going to let you discover he's married."

"I'd find out sooner or later."

"But what if later was too late?"

"As in she's already pregnant with the son they now have?"

"It could happen," said Tristan. "He's a wealthy guy. He buys a nice house in La Reina—"

Susannah and I cut him off with laughter.

"Okay," he said. "A nice house in Santa Fe. She visits him there. Falls in love with Santa Fe and then with Nomolos. She gets pregnant—"

"Before getting married?" asked Susannah. Then she looked at me and said, "Sorry, Hubie. I didn't mean to . . ."

Her voice trailed off. I said, "It's a legitimate question which could lead to an illegitimate situation. I see your point. But Sharice and I dated for three years before getting pregnant. And we knew each other for a few years before that. It was obvious neither of us had anything to hide. But maybe Nomolos and Madam X had a whirlwind romance in Santa Fe, ended up in bed, and she got pregnant." My imagination was in high gear now, so I kept adding to the oral novella. "He tells her he works up in the mountains. Sometimes he has to stay at the mine overnight. He tells his wife he has business in Santa Fe and has to stay overnight. He becomes a skillful bigamist."

"Except he isn't," said Susannah, "because he isn't married to Madam X."

"Why not?"

"Because you have to get a marriage license. And when he tried to get one, the fact that he is listed on the state rolls as currently married would pop up."

"No problem," says Tristan. "He finds some way to put off the wedding, like telling her they can't get a marriage license because she's a foreigner."

"There's no law against Americans marrying foreigners."

"She might not know that."

I said, "You know what we've just done? We've woven together a story of the Nomolos family without knowing whether a single thread of our creation is correct."

Susannah said, "We know some of it is true. We know he was married to the first woman. We know he has a housekeeper who looks like the son. We know he has a daughter that is concerned about what's going on. And we know he's dead."

"So where does that get us?" I asked.

40

I recounted my conversation with Susannah and Tristan to Sharice that evening.

"Makes sense," she said.

"Whit is still confused. And I'm a little bit confused myself. Probably because of the aliases we gave them or they gave themselves. If you ask me whether directions guy was Nomolos or Arcilla, I have to think about it for a few seconds to be sure."

"So what's next?"

"Someone has to figure out for certain whether Nomolos was murdered or accidentally poisoned. And if he was murdered, then someone has to figure out who did it."

"Isn't that supposed to be 'who done it?'"

I laughed. "A bookstore in Taos called Moby Dickens used to sponsor a book club called 'Who did it: A grammatically correct book club.'"

"Moby Dickens?"

"Yeah. The guy who owned it, Art Bachrach, had a great sense of humor and a great love of books."

"Past tense?"

"Sadly, yes. He died about ten years ago. The bookstore has a new owner and a new name, *Op. Cit.*"

"I'll bet Susannah can figure out what really happened. She's good at mysteries."

I nodded. "And it would be good for her to solve another one."

Being back in Sharice's condo felt good. I love the view of the Sandias and the lights of downtown. The interior is more sparse and hard-edge than my building in Old Town, but I've come to appreciate that look.

She saw me looking around and said, "Thinking again about where we should live?"

I nodded. "We have two good options, so we can't go wrong."

"Both options have the same challenge. One bedroom and one bathroom."

"That's not a problem in the short run," I said.

"Define short run."

"We haven't had any problem living with one bedroom and one bathroom. A crib doesn't require a separate room, and she'll probably be in a crib for three years."

"She or he," she corrected. "But do we want to move after three years? Wouldn't getting a permanent place when we get married and have a child make more sense? If so, shouldn't we do something about it now?"

"So we should choose downtown or Old Town now?"

"Or somewhere else?"

"Is there another area you like?"

"I like Nob Hill. Close to UNM. You can walk to restaurants and shops."

"You're right. And it's where I grew up. Maybe we could buy the house I grew up in."

"Too weird. How about the North Valley?"

"I like it. Especially if we had something close to the river. But it's a bit pricey up there."

"Corrales?"

"Love that little village, but I wonder if it's one of those great to visit but not to live."

"And getting to work would be more time and hassle."

"Right. Which puts us back to Old Town or downtown," she said. Then she added, "We can't enlarge the condo, but we could enlarge your place."

"I doubt it. The zoning in Old Town is rigorous."

"I'm not talking about changing the footprint of the building, just changing how the inside is arranged and used."

"How?"

She hesitated then said, "I don't want you to react quickly to what I'm about to say. Just think about it. The east third of the building has the shop, your pottery workshop, and the living area. We could turn the workshop into a second bedroom."

"Okay, I am not reacting; just clarifying. Where would I throw pots?"

"If you continue to serve as department head, you won't have time to throw pots."

"It's a temporary job."

"It was temporary for the spring. Now you're doing it for the summer and the fall."

"The fall will be my last semester."

"I think you're underestimating Dean Gangji's determination. He basically fabricated a graduate degree for you. He wouldn't do that just for you to be acting. He plans to make you the permanent head."

"You really think so?"

"How many deans go out to a bar to celebrate a temporary employee getting a degree?" She grinned and added, "Especially deans who are opposed to alcohol?"

Then the determinism thing popped into my mind again. I never sought the adjunct job. They needed a temporary person and happened to approach me. I never sought the acting head job, but I got it anyway. Was the permanent job somehow the next step in my employment destiny? If so, then why even worry about it? It was bound to happen. But if I didn't want it, could I avoid it? Not if it was determined. I felt that headache coming on and decided not to think about it. Or maybe fate prevented me from thinking about it.

Then Sharice said, "I'm going to take a shower; want to join me?" and I was back in my going-with-the-flow mode.

41

After Sharice left for work in the morning, I walked over to San Felipe de Neri Church.

The church was built in 1706, twenty-six years later than the building I live in.

The 1706 church collapsed in 1792 because there was so much rain that summer that the adobe disintegrated. That story seems to me and everyone else in Albuquerque to be some sort of myth concocted by the builder to escape being blamed for the collapse. Either that, or the planet has experienced a great deal of global drying.

The current church is also adobe. The walls are five feet thick, so short of a massive earthquake there is no danger it will collapse.

The same can be said of Father Groaz, the current priest at St. Neri. His craggy face, barrel chest, and bushy beard give him the look of a frontiersman, but as soon as he speaks, a different image comes to mind—Transylvania. His deep voice and Eastern European accent sound like an old Hollywood movie about vampires or werewolves. I actually enjoy his accent which makes my name sound like *Youbird*. He also often gives *s*'s a *z* sound, some *e*'s an *ea* sound, and some *o*'s a *u* sound, not to mention rendering the common *-ing* ending as *-nik*.

"Gud marnik, Youbird," he said when he spotted me approaching the bench he was sitting on. "Have you come for spiritual guidance?"

"I have. Or maybe *theological* is the more accurate word."

"Perhaps involves the little pot I see in the paper?"

Am I the only person in New Mexico who didn't see that? I think. I ask if he can tell me anything about the pot.

He points to the decoration that looks like this ה"ב and says, "Is Hebrew for 'with God's help.' Actually, is abbreviation, but is what it means, and is pronounced something like *B'ezrat HaShem*. But my Hebrew is even worse than my English, so do not rely on what I say."

"Is it used in any ceremony or ritual that involves candles?"

"It is used in many ways, usually about things that are about to happen in the future. For example, "With God's Help, Youbird will not consider converting to Judaism."

Then when he saw the puzzled look on my face, he burst into laughter. Then he said, "Maybe is used before some ritual begins, more or less seeking God's help, but not as part of ritual I am aware of."

"It isn't used in any way relating to a menorah?"

"There are two menorahs. One called simply *menorah* has seven candles and was the lamp used in the ancient holy temple in Jerusalem. A *Hanukkah menorah* has nine candles and is used only during Hanukkah. Eight of the candles are the same size. The ninth candle is different and is used only to light the other eight. I do not believe the phrase *B'ezrat HaShem* is used when lighting either type of menorah, but I am Catholic priest, not rabbi. May I ask what makes you curious about the pot?"

"This is a copy. The man who owned the original was murdered."

He crossed himself and muttered something under his breath. Then he asked me if the pot had some connection to the crime.

"I don't know. The man's name was Solomon, and I believe he was a crypto-Jew."

He smiled. "The Bishop tells me crypto-Jews are like Bigfoot, existing only in the imagination of the gullible."

"What do you think?"

"I keep open mind. Some parishioners tell me they fear a person related to them may be secretly following the Laws of Moses, and they want me to confront the person and bring them back into the Church. I tell them to bring the person to me, but they never do this."

"Tell me about King Solomon."

"This is related to crypto-Jews?"

"Maybe."

"Is a long story. God appeared to Solomon in a dream and said, 'Ask something of me and I will give it to you.' Solomon answered: 'God, you have made me, your servant, King to succeed my father David; but I am a mere youth, not knowing at all how to act. I serve you in the midst of the people whom you have chosen, a people so vast that it cannot be numbered or counted. Give your servant, therefore, an understanding heart to judge your people and to distinguish right from wrong.' Then God said to him, 'Because you have asked for this—not for a long life for yourself, nor for riches, nor for the lives of your enemies, but for understanding so that you may know how to rule wisely—I do as you requested. I give you a heart so wise and understanding that there has never been anyone like you up to now, and after you there will come no one to equal you.'"

"Yes," I said. "I associate Solomon with wisdom, the most famous example being two women both claiming to be the mother of a baby."

"You remember the details?"

"Sorry. It's been a long time since I read it."

"Is in Kings, chapter 3, verses 5 though 14. King Solomon was approached by two mothers who insisted they were the mother of the same child. One of them had accidentally smothered her baby in her sleep, and upon waking, had switched him with the baby of another woman living in the same house. That mother recognized the child was not hers, and tried to get her own baby back. Was a case of one word against another. Solomon said he will take a sword and slice the poor child in half, so that each mother can have half of the baby. One of the women likes the solution; she has no attachment to the child and, having lost her own baby, finds jealous comfort in knowing the other woman will also be unhappy. The other immediately cries out, begging the king to spare the child even if it means giving him up. So Solomon knows she is the real mother."

"It's a great story."

"Yes. But even though his forty-year reign is regarded as Israel's golden age, in the final years of his reign, he strayed from God. The Book of Deuteronomy warns kings and commands them not to do three things: 1) do not return to Egypt where the Jews were mistreated, 2) do not take many wives, and 3) do not accumulate large amounts of silver and gold. But Solomon broke all three of these commands. So God told him he would break up his kingdom. But out of respect for Solomon's father, David, he would wait until Solomon died before breaking up the kingdom. And even then, he would allow Solomon's son to keep one of the twelve tribes of Israel."

Then Father Groaz smiled and continued. "Solomon also created a very large central government and built very large government buildings including a big palace for him and his many wives. This required high taxes and conscripted labor and caused resentment among the Jews who preferred the historical tribal system which depended on local governance."

He paused there, smiled at me, and said, "Does it remind you of any government in modern times?"

I nodded. "The Israelites were probably the first taxpayers to mock the bureaucrats by making fun of them via the phrase, 'I'm from the central government, and I'm here to help you.'"

He laughed and then summed up the story. "The great and wise Solomon was once close to God's heart and preferred nothing of the world over God's wisdom. But the Solomon who died smothered in wealth, sex, and power was a different man, one whose heart had turned from God. Remember this quote from the *Book of Sirach*: 'Call no man happy before his death, for by how he ends, a man is known.'"

"There's a book called *Sirach* in the Bible?"

He laughed. "Is one of those secrets that Protestants claim we have." Then he laughed some more and said, "*Sirach* is actually part of the *Apocrypha*, a collection of books that were not included in the Bible."

42

Askance is not a word we get many chances to use, but it definitely describes the way Susannah looked at me after I told her about my conversation with Father Groaz.

"You thought maybe the Solomon's Mines guy in New Mexico was somehow reenacting the life of the Solomon who lived in Jerusalem two thousand years ago with his seven hundred wives and three hundred concubines?"

"Not consciously reenacting, but maybe influenced by. And we have to assume he was the one who named the mining company, so Solomon or the story of Solomon was important to him."

"Maybe he bought the mine from someone else and it already had that name."

"I don't think so."

She said she recognized the sly smile I had assumed and demanded I tell her why I didn't think Nomolos had bought the mine from someone else.

"Because we now know his real name is *Minero*, which means 'miner' in Spanish."

She brightened, "And he's one of those crypto-Jews who chose a common noun as a last name like *rueda*!"

"Exactly. And he chose *Minero* because that's what he had been in Spain, a miner. And do you remember what the conquistadores were most hoping to find in New Mexico?"

"Yes!" she said. "The Seven Cities of Cibola, a land of gold the Spanish of the 16th century believed existed somewhere in the southwest of North America, comparable to the better-known mythical city of El Dorado."

"Right." I said. "The four survivors of the disastrous Narvaez Expedition of 1527 were the first to mention Cibola. Coronado arrived in 1540 and looked for Cibola but never found it."

She displayed a phony smile and said, "Or maybe Coronado found the seven cities and kept it secret so that only he and his men could split the loot."

"And maybe our friend Nomolos Minero bought one of the Cities of Gold from a descendent of Coronado."

"And then bought a shopping mall and named it after Coronado!"

After we stopped laughing, she became suddenly serious and said, "Who killed Minero, Hubie?"

"I don't know. But I think you can figure it out."

43

Juneteenth," said Sharice.

I told her I'd never heard of it. We were at Dos Hermanas with Susannah and Freddie, both of whom admitted they had never heard of it either.

Sharice said, "On June 19, 1865 in Galveston, a proclamation from President Lincoln was read freeing all slaves in Texas. That day, June nineteenth, is now celebrated as Juneteenth to commemorate emancipation and to recognize the struggle for freedom and equality of African Americans."

"So our wedding will be on the day slavery ended?" I asked.

"Juneteenth is the day my father chose for the wedding," she said. "Most Canadians probably never heard of it, but my father is a student of Black history. And he'd be the first to tell you that slavery didn't end that day. There was still slavery in Maryland, for example, because they had stayed in the Union, so Lincoln looked the other way."

"Another place where it didn't come to an end," I said, "was right here in New Mexico."

"Why did it not end here?" asked Sharice.

"After the conquistadores enslaved the Pueblos, the Spaniards continued to raid other tribes well into the 1800s, taking Apaches, Comanches, and especially Navajos as slaves. During the years when New Mexico was a US territory, it was similar to the southern states in the US, a small aristocracy of landowners holding vast estates and a thriving economy that depended heavily on slave labor. During that time a handful of slaves freed in Texas moved to New Mexico. They were not re-enslaved because New Mexico didn't need them; they had plenty of Indian slaves. So New Mexico was a better option for the former Texas slaves than staying in Texas."

She looked at me and said, "I remember a story you told me about one of those freed slaves. The famous cattleman John Chisum was living in Texas when the Civil War began, and he freed all his slaves on that very day. One of the slaves he freed was a woman named Jensie whom he had purchased from her previous owner because he thought the owner was mistreating her. Then he and Jensie were married and had two daughters who were Chisum's only descendents."

"True," I said, "although some people quibble about whether they were legally married because of course intermarriage was illegal in Texas at that time. But my view is they were married because they moved to New Mexico where interracial marriage was not illegal."

"Really?" asked Sharice.

"Actually it was legal only because the Territorial Legislature had never passed a law regarding it because there were so few Blacks in the territory. The only law in territorial New Mexico regarding Blacks was passed in 1856 and for the first time it put a quota on the number of free Blacks coming into New Mexico. It was clearly a discriminatory law, but one that made sense to them at the time. Texas had 250,000 slaves at the start of the war. The total population in New Mexico at that time was about 90,000. So I imagine the legislature was thinking that if all those slaves were freed and came to New Mexico, the New Mexicans already there would be outnumbered three to one. But the law was struck when New Mexico gained statehood." I looked at Sharice. "Good thing for me."

"We've come a long way," Susannah said.

"And we still have a way to go," said Sharice.

"One more item on this subject," I said.

Sharice laughed and said, "You're beginning to sound like a prof."

"Got that from my dad."

"Hey, I'm a prof," said Freddie.

Susannah elbowed him and said, "You're an adjunct just like me."

"Okay, I'm outnumbered," Sharice said. "Give us the one more item."

"The Thirteenth Amendment to the US Constitution abolished slavery and involuntary servitude throughout the nation. The inclusion of the term *involuntary servitude* was added specifically to eliminate New Mexico Territory's long tradition of indentured servitude."

"You know a lot about New Mexico's history," Sharice noted, "but very little about America's popular culture."

"Popular culture is ephemeral. I don't read newspapers or watch television because the stuff they talk about is forgotten a week later. I like hundred-year-old history, thousand-year-old pots, billion-year-old planets, and marriages that last forever."

Susannah teared up a bit. She's a rough and tumble cowgirl, but she has a soft heart.

"Juneteenth is in one of your categories," Sharice said with a roguish smile.

"History?"

"No. It's in with marriage because it will last forever. It's now officially Juneteenth National Independence Day, a federal holiday."

"When did that happen?" asked Freddie.

"June 17th, 2021," Sharice said. "A little less than a year ago."

"They couldn't have waited two days and declared it on the day itself?"

She laughed. "If they had waited, they wouldn't have been able to celebrate it."

"They enacted it and shut down the government two days later?"

"Sort of. The implementation was typical of government inefficiency. Federal employees received a holiday but didn't find out about it until two hours before their workday started. The Post Office ignored it. A spokesperson said, "Closing down our operations without providing appropriate time would lead to operational disruptions."

"So everything in New Mexico will be closed on the day we get married?" I said. "That's great. We can invite the whole state to our wedding!"

44

Susannah called me a few days later and told me she had arranged a meeting at the church in La Reina.

"With whom and for what reason?"

"With Father Jerome, all four members of the family formerly known to us by the name Nomolos, Whit Fletcher, Triple T, Charles Webbe, and Layton Kent. You and Tristan are welcome to join us."

I must have lapsed into a brief stupor, because the next thing I heard was, "Hubie? Are you still there?"

I told her I was. A dozen questions were running laps in my mind, and the one I asked first for no reason was, "Layton agreed to this?"

"He did."

Then I realized there *was* a reason why I asked about Layton first. I figured he was the only person on the list of attendees who never does anything without thoroughly checking it out. If he had agreed to go, the meeting was important.

Layton Kent is the most prominent attorney in Albuquerque, in part because his client list reads like the Who's Who of New Mexico, and in part because his wife Mariella is said to be descended from Don Francisco Fernandez de la Cueva Enriquez, *Duque de Alburquerque*, the man after whom our city is almost named. I say *almost* because, as you may have noticed, the first *r* is missing.

Since I am neither prominent nor descended from royalty, you may wonder why I am on his client list. The answer is simple: Mariella is a discriminating collector of ancient pottery, and I am her primary source for those goods.

Layton has an office of course. As you might suspect, it is on the top floor of the Albuquerque Plaza Office Tower, the tallest building in Albuquerque. A status not unlike being the tallest dwarf in the world since it is only 350 feet tall.

The views from Layton's office include the Sandia Mountains to the east, the Sangre de Cristo Mountains to the north, and if you crane your neck, the heavens above.

But the view Layton most prefers is from his table overlooking the eighteenth green of the exclusive club he belongs to, and that is where I go when I have reason to meet with him.

I asked Susannah what the purpose of the meeting was.

"I'm going to ferret out the circumstances of the death of Abadias Minero, the owner—before he died—of Solomon's Mines. The meeting is scheduled for this afternoon at 2:00. And don't forget to bring Tristan if he wants to come. He might enjoy it."

Then she hung up.

I held the receiver in front of me. For those of you who don't know what a receiver is, it's the part of a traditional phone that you pick up out of its cradle and speak into when you get a call. I stared at it. I don't know why people used to do that, but it was a common thing after a puzzling call, and this one certainly qualified.

Then I remembered Susannah asking me "Who killed Minero, Hubie?"

To which I responded, "I don't know. But I think you can figure it out."

45

When I told Tristan about the meeting, he said he wanted to be there to see how things would unfold.

I feared *unfold* might be the wrong verb. Given that the meeting included three law enforcement people, four people who might be the murderer of Abadias Minero, a lawyer, and a cowgirl with Nancy Drew as an alter ego, the verb that came to me was not *unfold*—it was *unravel*. I just hoped the presence of Father Jerome might be a steadying influence.

As we drove north, Tristan asked, "Does the fact that Whit and Triple T are there mean they're going to arrest someone?"

"I have no idea. I don't even know why Whit would be there. Abadias Minero wasn't murdered in Albuquerque."

"Maybe there's some money to be split up," he said and laughed.

We were the last to arrive, but it was obvious the meeting hadn't begun. Father Jerome and Triple T were moving some chairs around, and a few people were taking off their coats.

When the chairs were lined up facing the front pew, Father Jerome asked the Minero family to sit together in the pew. The rest of us sat in the chairs facing them.

Triple T seemed both impressive and approachable, a perfect blend for a law enforcement officer. His wavy hair showed a touch of silver as did his neatly-trimmed moustache. His blue jeans had a perfect crease and fit snugly over the uppers of his cowboy boots. The leather of his belt matched the boots. There was a badge on the tan sports coat, a string tie on the white shirt, and a smile on his weathered brown face. Take off the badge, and he'd be casted as the perfect grandfather in a Disney film.

He began with introductions. "Thanks to all of you for coming. The people in the pew are Mrs. Maymona Minero, her daughter Lauri Biegler Minero, Elia Saavedra, and her son Abraam Minero."

Ole Triple T, as Whit calls him, may be a backcountry sheriff, but he was not only dressed well, he was also what we call pretty *vivo* out here. I guess the closest English word is *savvy*.

I admired the way his simple introduction conveyed in a subtle and nonjudgmental way the facts that Maymona was married to the deceased and mother of the daughter, and Elia was *not* married to the deceased and was mother to the son.

Then he introduced Whit by saying, "All of the out-of-towners are from Albuquerque. The only one I knew before today is seated at the opposite end of the chairs down there. He's Detective First Class Whit Fletcher of the Albuquerque Police Department, and I'll let him introduce the others."

Whit's shiny silver suit had a bulge on the left chest that I knew was his Smith & Wesson 357 Magnum Highway Patrolman Model. The APD had assigned him a Glock automatic, but he told me he preferred a revolver because they never jam. I merely report this as told to me. I know almost nothing about guns, and even that is too much.

He began by thanking Triple T for helping to organize the meeting and Father Jerome for hosting it. Then he did the introductions: "Next to me is Layton Kent, a big shot attorney from Albuquerque." He turned to Layton and said, "You want me to tell them about all the awards and recognitions you've received over the years?"

Layton gave a wan smile and said, "'Big shot' was more than enough, Detective Fletcher."

Whit continued, "Next to Mr. Kent is Miss Susannah Inchaustigui, a professor at the University of New Mexico whose specialty is religious symbolism. Next to Professor Inchaustigui is Mr. Hubie Schuze, owner of Spirits in Clay, a retail pottery establishment in Old Town. Next is Tristan Logand, Mr. Schuze's nephew, and last is Charles Webbe from the FBI."

All eyes turned to Webbe. Just what I expected. At six-three and two hundred twenty-five with a waist no larger than mine, he was impressive in his dark blue suit, white shirt and conservative striped tie.

Whit continued. "The reason we got all you folks together is to discuss the death of Abadias Minero. I will refer to him as Abadias so as not to confuse him with his son who is also Mr. Minero. In fact, I'll just call everyone by their given names to make things easier and more friendly-like.

"Because Abadias was not a resident of Albuquerque, you may wonder why all of these people from the Duke City are here. The short answer is that all of them had some sort of connection with Abadias. Let me lay it out for you in brief. Tristan was hired by Abadias to use a 3-D printer to make eight copies of a ceramic pot. He made an extra one and gave it to his Uncle Hubie who's in the pottery business. A reporter for Channel 17 did a report about the pot on the air. That report also got printed in the *Albuquerque Journal.* After that report, Abadias visited Hubie's pottery shop and asked directions to a local café frequented by Hubie. Later that evening, Hubie saw him there. But of course he wasn't surprised by that since he had given him directions. At that point, Hubie didn't know that the stranger asking for directions was Abadias. But I think we can safely assume that Abadias going into Hubie's shop was not a coincidence. He wanted to take a look-see, maybe see if the pot was on display.

"Not long after that, Abraam also went to Hubie's shop and inquired about the pot. Then Lauri did the same thing." Whit paused for a moment and looked at each of the family members. Then he said, "We think the pot had something to do with Abadias' death. So we want each of you to give a summary of events beginning with the decision of Abadias to have the pots copied and running all the way up to when he died."

He looked at Maymona Minero and said, "I'd like you, Mrs. Minero, to go first seeing as how you're the oldest in the family.

Sorry for not callin' you by your first name, but I don't know how to pronounce it."

In addition to Triple T and Whit being on opposite ends of the chairs facing the pew, they were also on opposite ends of the *savoir faire* spectrum.

Maymona Minero had sat motionless on the pew, her eyes focused on something behind us. The only indication that she had heard Whit was that she began to speak.

"My husband inherited that little pot from his father who had inherited it from his father and so on. He was proud that it had come from Spain and had been in his family for many centuries. It was a tradition that the Minero son who received the pot would drink wine from it on Friday at sundown. When Abraam got old enough to be interested in adult matters, he began to ask a lot of questions about the routines and practices of our family. Abraam used the internet to find answers his father would not or could not give him. He discovered that the true purpose of the pot was not for wine. It was supposed to be a candle in a special candleholder made with precious metal that held eight other candles. His father finally agreed to construct such a candleholder. That was when he hired Mr. Logand to make eight copies, and also when Abadias began to build the candleholder. When the candleholder was complete, he announced that we would have a special ceremony on Friday at sundown. He would drink wine from the old pot for the last time. Then he would fill it with oil, insert a wick, and light it. It would then be used to light the other eight candles."

She took a handkerchief from her purse. "He said the special words he always said when he drank the wine. They are in some other tongue that I do not understand. Then he drank the wine. When the pot was empty, he placed it on the table, filled it with oil, and lit it. At that point he asked Abraam to light the rest of the candles. Abraam was almost finished when his father suddenly took an awkward step forward as if he had tripped, and then he fell to the floor. I rushed over to help, but he was unconscious. Abraam was also by his side and listened for a heartbeat. There wasn't one. Abraam rolled his father over and tried pumping his chest to restart his heart. But it quickly became obvious that it was too late."

She dabbed at her eyes with the handkerchief. "After we were positive he had died, we decided the best thing to do was call the sheriff. He would know the proper steps to take from there. But Abraam said his father would not want an outsider involved, especially on a Friday evening with the candleholder in plain sight. Even though we had been married for many years, I was not certain what Abadias would have preferred, so I agreed to not calling the sheriff. And so did Elia. Lauri suggested we take Abadias to the church. We are not Catholics, but she said it was the right place because it was open, it was a holy place, and Father Jerome would know the right steps to take. So that's what we did."

Whit said, "When Abadias' body got to the State Medical Examiner's office he had some things in his pocket but no wallet."

Mrs. Minero said, "His wallet had company credit cards, the combinations to the safes, a bunch of business cards from suppliers, agents, and buyers, safety deposit box keys, and all sorts of other things. Rather than take time to sort through everything, we decided just to keep the wallet and sort things out later."

"What I figured," said Whit. Then he turned to Elia. "I'm afraid I can't pronounce your name either. But I'd like you to tell me if there's anything you would like to add, subtract or change in what we just heard."

"No. Her description of the events that evening is as I remember them."

Whit asked the same question of Lauri and Abraam and got the same answer from both.

Either Mrs. Minero's summary was correct or they had all agreed to the same cover story.

Abadias Minero didn't die of natural causes. He died from sodium cyanide, a very fast-acting poison. So it was obvious the poison was in the cup he drank from. And the most likely explanation of how it got there was that one of the other people in the room that night had put poison in the cup or the wine.

Of course Whit knew what I knew and concluded what I concluded. So he scanned each of the four faces on the pew and said, "It's nice that you all remember the events exactly the same. And also kind of amazing. I've been a cop for thirty years and never had four witnesses agree on every detail. Now you'd think having all the witnesses agree would make a cop's job easier. But what it does for this old cop is make me suspicious. Because Abadias was poisoned with sodium cyanide which acts real fast. So the poison had to be in that little cup. And that means someone in that room that night murdered Abadias."

They were all stone-faced.

Whit said, "Anybody got anything to say?"

Of course he was asking the four people in the Minero family, but I was the one who spoke up. "I think I know what happened," I said.

Whit turned to face me. "I was asking them."

"They aren't answering because they don't know what happened. I do."

"How could you know? You weren't even there."

"I wasn't there, but I have some information no one knows about."

"Let's hear it."

I looked at Mrs. Minero. "Your husband was using gold in building that candleholder wasn't he?"

"Yes."

"And he was using sodium cyanide in the process."

"Yes."

"You worked with your husband in this business for a long time. Can you give us a brief explanation of how sodium cyanide is used?"

"We crush the gold ore into a fine powder. Then we add the sodium cyanide to the powder. The cyanide binds to the gold ions which allows us to separate the gold from the ore."

"How much gold would he be using on the candleholder project?"

"Just a little. Making the whole candleholder out of gold would have taken way too much gold. He was only coating the little circles where the pots would sit."

"Thank you. Father Jerome, you told me that you saw the little cup in the workshop, right?"

"I did."

"Lauri, you were often in the office when your father was making the candleholder, correct?"

"Yes."

"And the workshop is visible from the office?"

"Yes."

"Tell us what you saw regarding the little cup."

"He used the little cup to hold the cyanide."

"Why did he use the cup?"

"He said there were two reasons. First, it was almost exactly the small size he needed. Second, it was symbolic that the pot would be used in the construction of the candleholder it would be a part of. Symbolism was important to him."

"Didn't he think putting cyanide in the cup was dangerous?"

"Of course he knew cyanide is dangerous. But he had worked with it for years, and he knew how to safely handle it. He was very careful to wipe the cup dry each time after he poured out the cyanide. He even discarded the rag he wiped the cup with and used a clean rag to wipe it again after the next pour."

"How many pours were there?"

"Sixteen. Two for each candle in the candleholder."

It seemed to me that people were now sitting up straighter. So it seemed the right time to spring my story on them.

"I'm not a metallurgist or a chemist. I'm just a humble potter. But I know that little pot was unglazed. And I know unglazed clay absorbs liquids. And wiping the inside doesn't remove what is absorbed. I doubt there was enough cyanide absorbed into that pot after the first time he filled it to kill anyone. But it takes very little cyanide to do so, and after absorbing sixteen portions of cyanide, that pot's unglazed wall was full of the stuff. You can't wipe out things absorbed into clay. The only way to get them out is to put liquid into the cup and let the absorbed stuff seep back out. And that's exactly what happened when Abadias poured wine into the pot. The sixteen pours of cyanide that had each partially seeped into the clay came back out into the wine. He died of accidental poisoning."

I'm corny enough to say "you could have heard a pin drop" except you couldn't have because Mrs. Minero was wailing.

Layton Kent stepped over to her side and put his arm around her. I'd never seen him display that sort of emotion, and I suddenly felt good about having him as my lawyer.

He leaned down and whispered something to her. She whispered something back. He hugged her.

While Layton was with Mrs. Minero, Charles Webbe was talking to Elia.

Triple T suggested we all take a brief break. He, Whit, Charles, and Layton went with Father Jerome into the priest's office.

The four family members huddled in a corner of the church and whispered.

Tristan, Susannah, and I remained in our chairs.

Susannah asked me *sotto voce*, "Did you make up that stuff about absorption?"

"No. That's really how unglazed clay works."

"Wouldn't Minero have known that?"

"He worked with metal, not clay. Metal doesn't absorb. Clay does."

46

Triple T, Whit, Charles, and Father Jerome returned from their meeting and asked us all to resume our places.

Triple T was the first to speak. "What we have here is a tricky situation. Detective Fletcher, Agent Webbe, and I all agree that the preponderance of evidence points to an accidental poisoning. Both a priest and a family member were witness to the pot being used in the workshop. The timing of the death shortly after the deceased drank from the cup is consistent with what we know about cyanide. And there is no evidence that contradicts the accidental poisoning explanation. However, a case could be made that some or all of the family members had a motive. Now please bear with me on what I am about to say. I'm not accusing anyone. I believe the death was accidental. However, the death will have to be examined by the forensic pathologist from the office of the Medical Investigator who will determine the manner and cause of death. A detective would include those findings in his report, and would doubtless also include information suggesting that some or all of the family members had a motive. The district attorney would then decide whether to charge anyone in relation to Abadias' death.

"As I say, this is difficult, but I have to spell out what the district attorney might think. Mrs. Minero had a motive because Abadias was unfaithful. Ms. Saavedra had a motive because Abadias did not divorce his wife before fathering a child with Ms. Saavedra. Lauri may fear that her father was going to leave the mine to the son. Abraam may fear that if Mrs. Minero inherits the mine, she would eventually leave the mine to her daughter because Abraam is not her birth child.

"I am not saying that any of you have those thoughts or motives. I'm merely saying the authorities may think you have them. So, after talking it over with Detective Fletcher and Mr. Kent, we have a suggestion for you to consider."

Triple T sat and Layton Kent stood, a position in which he was quite imposing, what with his eighth of a ton inside a two-thousand-dollar hand-tailored suit.

He held up a paper. "Mrs. Minero informed me that her husband did not have a will. I have drafted a document that can be used in lieu of a will. It is an agreement among all four of the family members here that they will each receive twenty-five percent of Abadias Minero's worldly possessions. This document serves three purposes. First, and most important, it helps ensure that the detective will not dispute the recommendation of three law enforcement agents—Sheriff Todero, Agent Webb, and Detective Fletcher—that the death be classified as accidental poisoning. Because all four family members get an equal share, no one benefits by murdering Abadias to get an inheritance. Second, it relieves the four of you from haggling over who gets what."

Lauri frowned and said, "We would not haggle over who gets what."

Layton nodded and said, "I'm certain all four of you feel that way now. But I have handled hundreds of estates in my career, and what starts off as a friendly meeting to distribute the assets often turns ugly, pitting family members against each other. Let me explain to you why that might happen. New Mexico is what we call a 'modified community property state.' A normal community property state is one in which all the property of a married couple is considered to be held jointly and equally by both husband and wife. When either spouse dies, the other spouse inherits everything unless there are adult children. In that case, the adult children share half of the estate, and the surviving spouse gets the other half. But

New Mexico has one difference which makes it a *modified* community property state, and that modification is that the community property is not everything; it is only the assets acquired during the marriage. Assets belonging to a spouse before the marriage are separate and do not pass automatically to the surviving spouse. That means in this case, the mine—which Abadias Minero owned before he married—would not automatically go to his wife. Since that is the largest asset by far, deciding who gets it could lead to heated disputes. Another complication is that Abraam is—please excuse the use of the phrase, but it is still the legal term—an illegitimate child. All fifty states grant an illegitimate child the right to inherit from their mother because parenthood in that case is certain, but states do not presume that the child is the legal child of their father. So Abraam could be left with nothing if the estate goes to probate. I believe you are all of good will at this trying time, but if the estate goes to probate, problems could arise. Agent Webbe, I believe you want to comment."

Charles stood and said, "Ms. Elia Saavedra has given me permission to share this information with those present, some of who are already aware of it. I did some checking before coming to this meeting and discovered that Ms. Saavedra is in this country illegally. She entered the US on a tourist visa which has now been expired for years. If the estate goes to probate and she participates even indirectly through a lawyer, her whereabouts will be known to the Department of Homeland Security, and she may be deported."

Abraam said, "You now know my mom is here, so she'll be deported anyway."

Charles shook his head. "It is not my job to enforce visa violation. That is for the Department of Homeland Security. And I have not and will not tell them anything."

All four members of the family nodded.

Layton stood again, smiled, and said, "The third good thing about this document is it saves you a very large legal expense because Father Jerome asked me to donate my services."

He gave each member of the family a copy, and suggested that we leave them alone to discuss it amongst themselves.

47

Turns out Layton and Susannah had carpooled to La Reina, although I'm sure Layton would never use the term *carpool*. Sounds too blue-collar.

And of course they had travelled in his Rolls. I can't imagine him in Susannah's old beat-up Ford.

The trip and the meeting had taken a lot out of me, both physically and mentally. Tristan drove the Bronco on the way home, and I stared out at the mountains. I got a glimpse of Jicarita Peak off to the east and remembered that a rough map discovered on the bodies of two dead prospectors launched rumors about a hidden gold mine up there. There are some great hiking trails there. Most people walk them for the exercise and the views. But some are still looking for that mine.

Sharice made me a salad of nuts, fruits, and greens because I was too tired to wait for something to be cooked.

The next morning, I walked to work, sat behind the counter, and finished *Sky Determines*. On my last trip to the library, I'd checked out a book titled *Unleavened Dead*, in part because I was thinking about the crypto-Jews, in part because it's a murder mystery and I knew Susannah would like it, and in part because the author is Rabbi Ilene Schneider.

The only other woman rabbi I'd heard of was Rabbi Lynn Gottlieb here in Albuquerque who founded Congregation Nahalat Shalom. Like Rabbi Schneider, Rabbi Gottlieb was one of the first women to become a rabbi. She is also a human rights activist, writer, visual artist, and community educator.

I sold a small pot. There were more tourists now that school was out, and that's why my sales are best in the summer months.

You know where I went at five, and you know who was there.

The first words out of Susannah's mouth were, "How did you know Lauri had seen her father fill the cup with cyanide?"

I gave her a smile that I suspect made me look like the Cheshire cat. "I didn't know she'd seen her father fill the cup with cyanide for the very good reason that she didn't."

"Then why did she say she did?"

"Because I told her that if Abadias had been seen using the pot to hold cyanide, his death might be ruled an accident."

"When did you tell her that?"

"She had told Tristan she might come back and talk to the owner, and she did. She was quite surprised to discover that I was the guy who had dropped in on her at the office of Solomon's Mines. She told me the four members of the family had argued over who killed Abadias, and no one would admit it. So they decided when questioned that they would all tell the same story about the night he died. And they also agreed that no one would accuse anyone. But you knew that, didn't you?"

She blushed. It's something she almost never does, mainly because she's so honest and straightforward that she never feels she's done anything that would require a blush.

"How did you know I knew?"

"Because when you told me you were going to solve Abadias' murder, I figured you must have talked to the family. And you had arranged a meeting, which also required you to talk to them."

"So we were working at cross-purposes," she said. "I advised them to stick to their story, but you told Lauri to lie about the pot being in the workshop."

"No. Turns out our two approaches were not at cross-purposes; they were complementary. They all needed to tell the same story so that the murder couldn't be pinned on any one of them with certainty. But adding the possibility that it was an accident makes it easier for them to stick to the story, especially if no one is charged. And I don't know with absolute certainty that Lauri lied."

"But you told her to."

"No. I told her that *if* the pot had been seen being filled with cyanide, it might cause the investigating detective to rule the death an accident."

"Sounds like a politician wriggling out of a lie."

"Except they're better at it because they've had more practice."

"Well, since you know I talked to the family and set up the meeting, you might as well know what else I did."

She took a sip of her margarita looking at me over the rim of the glass.

"What else did you do?"

"I called Arcilla to get more information about his meeting with the Mineros before I called the family."

I thought for a few seconds then remembered her staring at his number when I showed her the slip of paper and she correctly guessed the first two numbers were the country code for Spain. She had stared because she was memorizing the number. Okay, she knew the number. But she didn't know Spanish. And I was confident she also didn't know Galician or Hebrew. So I asked her how she and Arcilla were able to talk.

"Simple. My phone has an app that translates as I speak."

Sometimes I feel like an alien on my own planet.

Susannah said, "Arcilla—I think I'll keep calling him that—told me when he got back that he started asking around about people from his village who had left unaccountably, and he discovered one."

"Elia Saavedra," I guessed.

"Right. She was in an abusive marriage and had to get out."

"But she didn't have enough money to just go away and live. So when she saw the online message from Minero, she jumped at it?"

She said, "That's what I figured. Minero was no bargain. He was married for heaven's sake! But he was better than what she left. He never hit her. She had a home, food, clothes, and other things people need. And she has a son she adores. And if all goes well, she'll own one fourth of a gold mine. Oh, and I have a surprise for you. But I won't spoil it by telling you now."

48

The wedding was nearing. All I had to do was wait and do what I was told.

Sort of like getting a Master of Fine Arts degree.

Sharice, her father, and Susannah were planning everything.

I was selling a few pots.

Lauri made another trip to Spirits in Clay.

She told me there might be a problem with the investigating detective, and then asked me how certain I was that the old clay pot would absorb cyanide.

"One hundred percent."

"How certain are you it would absorb enough to kill someone?"

"Less than a hundred percent. Maybe sixty percent. I looked up sodium cyanide in my encyclopedia. Based on how little it takes, there's certainly enough space in the wall of that cup to hold a lethal amount. When I first got the idea, I ran an experiment to make sure my theory was plausible. I filled my copy with red wine, let it sit for a while, and then poured it out. Then I let it sit over-night. The next day I poured water into the cup and let it sit until the afternoon. The water was almost as dark as the wine, so it had leeched out. What is the problem with the detective?"

"He told us he is almost ready to rule the death an accidental poisoning, but there is one last test he wants to run just to be sure."

"The same test I ran except with cyanide instead of wine and using scientific measuring techniques?"

"Exactly. And he's coming by to pick up the cup tomorrow."

Neither one of us had ever said anything outright about the fact that we had fabricated the story. I suppose the main reason is people don't like to admit to lying, which is proven every time someone tells one lie to cover another one. But the second reason is that the story could be true. Abadias liked tradition, ceremony, and symbolism. The cup had been in the workshop at one point. We had Father Jerome's word on that, and he was not likely to lie. Of course he saw it before the menorah project, but at least we knew the cup had been in the workshop once, so it wouldn't be a shock if it was in there more than once.

"What do you suggest?" I asked her.

"I suppose it's possible that you brought your pot to the big meeting in the church."

"Sure. That's certainly possible."

"And it's a dead-ringer for the original. So if the two pots were sitting there when you left the church, you might have picked up the wrong one."

"I'm not the most observant guy in the world. I've been known to lock my keys in my Bronco and leave my jacket in my office overnight."

"So if, as I hand the detective the pot, I should happen to notice that it's your copy and not the original, I suppose he would then come here and ask you for the original."

It was obvious at this point that Lauri had led the family to the shared story plan. And that she was an intelligent and well-spoken person.

"No doubt that is what the detective would do," I said. "And he will likely be disappointed that I threw what I thought was my copy of the pot into the Rio Grande because I was fed up with all the events having to do with a cup that caused me a great deal of angst."

She smiled and handed me the original cup. I gave her my copy.

She also gave me a paper I had asked for granting me the right to make copies of the little pots. Then I realized that if I made copies, it might be a bit tricky to explain to the detective why I threw away one. Oh well, I'd come up with a plausible story. I was getting good at that.

Then she gave me a box with a bow on the top. "This is a little present for you for all your help you gave my family."

It was a Crater Candle made from ashes taken from a crater formed over eighty million years ago near what is now the town of Wetumpka, Alabama.

"I thought a candle would be an appropriate gift," she said.

"It is, indeed. But why one from Wetumpka?"

"Because the man whose last name is my middle name is an archaeologist, and he travelled to Wetumpka to do a survey of ancient Native American sites. He brought several candles back as souvenirs."

Since Lauri and I were now co-conspirators and maybe even friends, I told her about the story Susannah, Tristan, and I concocted about how her father met Elia Saavedra.

"I'm curious to know if we were close to the truth."

She laughed. "You were very close. The only thing you missed was that my father flew to Galicia to meet her in person after they met online. The two of them came back together. Dad said Elia would be our housekeeper and also a connection with our family's roots. When it became obvious that Elia was pregnant, Mom and I assumed she had been pregnant when Dad hired her and that he didn't know because she wasn't showing. But after Abraam was born, the true situation was obvious to us."

She hesitated for a moment. "It was difficult for all of us."

I nodded.

Her natural smile returned, and she said, "For all the pain it caused my mother and me, my father bringing Elia into the family did lead to some good things. Dad wouldn't listen to Elia when she tried to instruct him about Judaism. He was not a listener. But Abraam learned about Judaism from his mother, and Dad did listen to Abraam. That's why Dad agreed to build the menorah and stop using the little pot for wine. I've gotten over the fact that he cared more about his son than he did about me. It's hard to hold a grudge against someone who's dead."

"Did you know my nephew saw a pistol in your purse when you came here the first time?"

She blushed. "No. I rarely think about the pistol. I carry it because thieves think a gold mine is a good place to rob. Gold can't be traced and it's easy to sell."

I thought about all the places in Albuquerque with a sign saying they buy gold and silver.

I called Susannah and told her about Lauri's visit and the plan we hatched.

"Don't throw the original into the river," she said.

"You have a better idea about how to get rid of it?"

"I do. I'm coming right over. Hang on."

She was there in less than five minutes because she was working a shift at La Hacienda where she was still filling in as a server when they were shorthanded.

"Gimme the pot," she said.

I did. "It's extremely important that the detective investigating Abadias Minero's death never see it," I said.

"I know that. Trust me. Got to get back quick. Party of eight wants their check. Could be a good tip."

49

I called Whit and told him we needed that 3-D printer he said he could get his hands on. When he brought it, I called Tristan and told him the 3-D printer was in my shop, and he came over about an hour later and set up the printer and made copies.

Whit watched the printer make the first copy then said, "Ain't that something?"

I nodded in agreement. But we hadn't seen anything yet.

Tristan had a flat piece of soft wood. Maybe balsa—I don't know much about wood. He asked me to sign my name in the wood using a common nail. He instructed me to press just hard enough so that my signature was engraved into the wood, but not hard enough to make it too deep. It took a few tries to get it the way he wanted it.

When he had a signature he thought would work, he ran the machine's stylus over the entire piece of wood running in straight lines very precisely from side to side. You could barely see the stylus dip when it crossed any part of my signature indention.

Then he very carefully turned the pot he had just made upside down in a muffin tin.

Whit said, "You gonna bake it?"

Tristan laughed and replied, "No. I need the muffin pan to hold the cup steady."

He stuffed some dense padding around the upturned pot, positioned the stylus, and started the machine.

Whit and I stared in disbelief as the machine etched my signature into the bottom of the pot. Then underneath my signature it etched a *1*.

"Where did the one come from? I didn't write in a one."

"I programmed that in. It'll put a two under the next one."

Whit and I just looked at each other and shook our heads.

Tristan then used his internet skills to place an advertisement in the *Albuquerque Journal*. He was even able to pay for it using my credit card.

The event being advertised was a pot sale. For a mere hundred dollars, the first one hundred customers could buy a signed and numbered copy of the famous pot that had recently been featured in the *Journal*.

50

The line ran out the door and along the sidewalk.

The publicity on television and the *Albuquerque Journal*, followed by the advertisement, had brought out a lot of buyers. I figured a few of them were interested in the history and/or the design of the pot. But most of them were betting on the pots becoming valuable to collectors because there would be only a hundred of them. Later that afternoon, pots 1, 97, 98, 99, and 100 were the only ones left. I could have sold them all, but as we approached the end of the run, I went out, counted to the person in line who would get number 96, and told another fib; namely, that he was customer one hundred, and those behind him might as well go home. They were disappointed but took it well. Many of them shook the last buyer's hand as they left and congratulated him on his good fortune. Of course when he came in, we gave him pot 100, and he left a satisfied customer.

I gave pots 97, 98, and 99 to Whit, Susannah, and Tristan. Knowing the importance of my attorney and my best customer, I set aside pot 1 for Mariella Kent.

Then I hid a stack of bills totaling $4,100 in my secret compartment.

If you did the math for the pot sale, you know gross income was $9,600. I gave $2,500 dollars to Sharice to cover wedding expenses.

I chose that amount because her father was also pitching in $2,500, and evidently five thousand was barely enough to cover a wedding dress, rings, gratuities to the clerics who would be involved, a reception, and other miscellaneous items. Handing over $2,500 was preferable to having to be involved in the planning.

I gave Tristan $2,000 for summer school tuition, and I gave Whit a thousand for furnishing the 3-D printer, for helping up north which was out of his jurisdiction, and because it's always good to have a cop who can help you get out of jams.

51

Juneteenth was the day the slaves gained their freedom and I lost mine.

It would have been funny back in the days when men who were getting married were teased about losing their freedom.

Thankfully, those days are gone. Wedding the woman you want to spend the rest of your life with is the best day of a man's life.

And Mother Nature seemed to agree. The temperature was in the high seventies, perfect for my dark suit. My groomsmen—in alpha order so as not to show favoritism—were Emilio, Freddie, Martin, and Tristan. The five of us had gone to Suits Unlimited over on Menaul Boulevard and bought four identical suits for $199 each. Which all combined was less than half the tab for Sharice's gown. It was from Vera Wang, but it didn't put much of a dent in the wedding budget because it was a dress she already owned, a silver high-neck dress of crinkled chiffon with a slanting hemline. She did have a local seamstress make a slight adjustment to the line where the dress flared, moving it up a few inches so that it was not uncomfortably tight where there was the small baby bulge. Because the hem was already on the bias, the dress did not appear to be altered.

I thought silver was a nice compromise between traditional white and the new tradition that if it is not the bride's first wedding, she should wear pink, blue, or some other colored gown.

It was Sharice's first wedding, but perhaps the fact that she was with child influenced her choice of gown. But I doubt it. She does what she thinks is right rather than following an outdated tradition.

And this one is definitely an outdated custom. A groom who's been married five times can wear the same thing at wedding six that he wore at wedding one. Although he also might need to have the waist let out a bit, and not for so healthy a reason as having a child.

The wedding would take place in the gazebo on the Old Town Plaza. The participants were beginning to gather in Spirits in Clay. Susannah as Sharice's maid of honor, Mariella Kent and Miss Gladys as her bridesmaids, and Consuela as her Matron of Honor.

I was told there would be three officiants, whom I assumed would be Father Groaz from St. Neri in Old Town, Father Tully from the Episcopal Church, and a Seventh-day Adventist minister selected by Sharice's father.

But Susannah turned to me and said, "Sharice's dad was unable to find an SDA minister willing to participate, so the third officiant is the surprise I told you about. He's a cantor from Malpica de Bergantiños."

As I was wondering where Malpica de Bergantiños might be, I heard the sound of the front door opening and turned to see Alazar Minero, originally known to me as Arcilla.

He strode over and gave me a bear hug.

Before I could ask what was going on, Susannah said, "Line up folks. It's marriage time!"

52

The gazebo is the center of Old Town, a quirky construction with a hexagonal roof. Or maybe it's octagonal. There is so much gingerbread that it's hard to tell.

Something is usually happening under the gazebo, be it a band concert, a political debate, or—today—a wedding.

My wedding was like my MFA graduation. I did what I was told, felt a bit like I was floating through some sort of fantasy land, and remember only parts of it, putting a ring on Sharice's finger and kissing her being the two most memorable parts.

The three officiants led the procession to the music of a maria-chi band called *Los Lobos Solitarios* who were playing one of my favorite tunes—*Hermosa cariña* (*beautiful darling*).

Some of the lyrics are:

Preciosa regala
Del cielo ha llegado
No puedo evitarlo
Y quiero gritarlo

In English:

Precious gift
From heaven has come
I can't help it
I want to shout it

And at that point the singer let out a *grito fuerte* that may have been heard in La Reina, and there were shouts from the crowd in English, Spanish, and Spanglish.

The crowd included Dr. Santiago Batres and all the staff from his office where Sharice works. He is a great guy who provides free dental care for indigent residents of Albuquerque. And now he had given all his staff a day off with pay because they were at the wedding instead of the office.

Many of the staff from La Hacienda and Dos Hermanas were present. John Hoffsis from Treasure House Books and assorted other Old Town neighbors were there.

Whit Fletcher, Charles Webbe, Sheriff Todero, and Father Jerome were standing together. The entire Inchaustigui family was present. Gladwyn Farthing was there under a wide-brimmed hat for protection from the sun and was standing next to Layton Kent. Quite a few tourists were also watching. Everyone loves a wedding.

My groomsmen followed the mariachi band in the procession. They entered the gazebo, stood on the west side, and showed me where to stand.

Next in the procession came Sharice's attendants I already mentioned—Susannah as maid of honor, Mariella Kent and Miss Gladys as bridesmaids, and Consuela as Matron of Honor. They stood on the east side.

The band paused for a moment. Then on someone's signal, they played a piece by Wagner. You probably know it as *Here Comes the Bride*. If you've never heard it played by a mariachi band, you should do so. You can probably find it on your phone.

Sharice started her measured walk to the gazebo.

Okay, I admit it. I cried. Some would say it was not manly. I say it takes a real man to show emotion. The sight of Sharice, her father's hand on her elbow, approaching the gazebo where we would be married, had me reaching for a handkerchief which I didn't have. Freddie had one and slipped it to me.

Father Groaz began the ceremony. "Welcome friends and family of the bride and groom. We are gathered to celebrate their love by joining them in marriage. All of us need and desire to love and to be loved. And the highest form of love between two people is a monogamous committed relationship. Bride and Groom, your marriage today is the public and spiritual joining of your souls that have already been united as one in your hearts. Marriage will allow you a new environment to share your lives together, standing together hand in hand to face life and the world. Marriage will expand you as individuals, define you as a couple, and deepen your love for one another. To be successful, you will need strength, courage, patience and a very good sense of humor." Here there was scattered laughter.

Father Tully then said, "Who giveth this woman in marriage?"

"I, Collin Clarke, do giveth my daughter to this man, Hubert Schuze."

He took Sharice's hand, placed it in mine, and stepped back.

Father Tully then turned to me and said, "Repeat after me. I, Hubert Schuze, take you Sharice Clarke to be my lawful wife, to have and to hold, from this day forward, for better, for worse, for richer, for poorer, in sickness and in health, until death do us part."

I so repeated.

Then he turned to Sharice and, well . . . you know the drill. She said the same vows with different pronouns.

We exchanged rings.

We kissed.

Then Cantor Minero spoke. In Spanish, of course, so about half of the crowd understood him. Father Groaz translated to English for the other half.

Minero said, "A traditional Jewish wedding is held outside under a canopy. The Hebrew word for canopy is *chuppah*. I see this gazebo as a special *chuppah* for two special people. A second tradition is that both the bride—*kallah* in Hebrew—and the groom—*chatan* in Hebrew—have their heads covered. Our *kallah* has a lovely headpiece, and I have one for the *chatan*."

He pulled a yarmulke from his pocket and placed it on my head.

I wondered how long I could wear it before I would begin to have that little depressed ring in my hair.

"The final tradition," he said, "is the breaking of the glass."

He turned to Susannah, held out his hand, and she placed in it the little cup Lauri had brought to me. He wrapped it in a large handkerchief.

"The original meaning of the breaking of the glass was in remembrance of the destruction of the Temple. But today we may also see it as breaking the old taboos about who can marry whom. In the eyes of God, it does not matter what language you speak, what color your skin is, or whether you are rich or poor. What matters is you are grateful to God to have found the love of your life."

He placed the wrapped pot at my feet and said, "Demonstrate your virility!"

I stomped as hard as I could and heard the familiar (to me) sound of cracking clay, and then cheers including a few *mazel tovs.*

Minero picked up the handkerchief with the crushed pot in it, put the whole mess in his pocket, and whispered to me, "Susannah asked me to take this back to Spain."

Father Groaz then asked me to step next to my groomsmen and Sharice to step next to her bridesmaids.

Then he spoke to the assembled crowd. "Officiating at a wedding is the best part of my job. So today is a double pleasure for me because we have a second one. Would Mr. Eguzki Inchaustigui please join us in the gazebo?"

Although it was probably obvious to everyone else, I had no idea what was happening.

As Susannah's father approached, Sharice removed her veil and handed it to Susannah. Freddie took the flower out of my lapel and put it in his.

Only then did I realize what was about to happen.

The two of them stepped together in front of Father Groaz. Mr. Eguzki Inchaustigui gave his daughter's hand in marriage to Mr.

Frederick Blass. The couple exchanged rings and vows, and sealed everything with a kiss.

And I cried for the second time that day. My best friend, always unlucky in love, had found her true love, a new and better version of a man she had loved before.

I remember even less about the reception than I do about the wedding itself. Part of my confusion stems from the reception being in all the parts of Don Fernando Maria Arajuez Aragon's building. A buffet line of casseroles was on offer in Miss Gladys' Gift Shop. A bar was set up in F°ahrenheit F°ashions, and dessert (which consisted of several Basque burnt cheesecakes) was in Spirits in Clay.

Yes, burnt. On purpose. They definitely looked like someone had forgotten to set the timer on the oven.

Susannah said, "They're not burnt, Hubie. They're caramelized."

I shook my head. "They are well past caramelized. *Scorched* would be more accurate."

"Take a taste," she said.

I did. "It's delicious. And there's no crust."

She smiled. "Doing away with the crust makes the cheesecake creamier and softer."

"It's like an upside-down cake," I said. "The caramelized top is the crust!"

She laughed and told me that the Basque burnt cheesecake was named 2021's Flavor of the Year in the *New York Times*.

The Basque burnt cheesecake paired well with the cold Gruet being poured in F°ahrenheit F°ashions, and I made quite a few short trips between the two locales. Skipping the casseroles and stuffing myself with a sweet dessert and alcohol proved to be an unwise choice, but I didn't discover that until early the next morning.

53

Sharice and I opted not to have a honeymoon trip, choosing instead to use the money to convert the back half of Spirits in Clay into a suitable residence for a young couple with a child on the way.

The first order of business was to purchase a double bed. I know everyone loves queens and kings these days, but we didn't have space for a big bed. The two of us together weigh less than Layton Kent, and she and I are both 5'6", so a double is all we need. And I like having her as close to me as possible.

Martin is a good handyman. He was building a wall to separate the double bed and the foot-wide space around it from the rest of the living quarters which has the kitchen, dining table, and living area. Actually, the living area is now basically the dining chairs turned to face the courtyard.

Half the workshop would become a nursery, and the other half a walk-in closet. Sharice had pledged to use only 75 percent of the closet so that we could store our other meager belongings. My clothes would remain in what was originally a broom closet.

As Sharice had suggested, all my pottery supplies, tools, and wheel were now behind the counter in the shop. I wasn't sure I could work while on display, but I was willing to try. And I could always just hang a sheet between me and the window.

54

Susannah and Freddie had honeymooned in Lake Louise, and she showed me the pictures they took. I decided Canada was almost as beautiful as New Mexico. It just had a few too many trees in my opinion.

She was back and we were in Dos Hermanas looking at her pictures and drinking margaritas. Sharice was at work. Freddie was painting.

"That was quite a surprise you had for me. But surely Arcilla"— we were still calling him that—"didn't come all the way from Spain just to have me stomp on a clay pot."

"You're right. The real reason he came was to try and help the Minero family. When I told him Abadias had died, he asked if I thought it might be appropriate for him to contact them and ask if he could help. Evidently, Abadias never talked much about the crypto-Jewish thing. Maybe because he wanted to keep them in the dark or didn't understand it himself. Or both. After Abraam was born and learned about Judaism from his mother, Abadias did listen to him to some extent. At least enough to go along with the menorah plan. Arcilla said he might be able to help them sort out their beliefs and philosophies. He said he didn't care if they ended up going to a synagogue and being normal Jews, or if they became Catholics, or Taoists for that matter. The important thing was for them to find the spiritual path that was right for them. He called them and volunteered to be a guide for their journey. They were happy he wanted to help, and they invited him to visit."

"And you figured as long as he was here, he might as well take part in my wedding. And yours."

"Right. And then the original pot that contained cyanide poured into it by either Abadias or a member of his family needed to disappear. And so I saw Arcilla's return as an Act of God."

"It was predestined."

"Exactly. What better way to get rid of the pot than to stomp it to pieces and ship it off to Spain from whence it came?" She took a sip of her margarita and did that looking-over-the-rim thing she does so well.

I said, "There's something else, isn't there?"

She nodded. "I think Arcilla has a crush on Elia."

"Please tell me he's not married."

"He told me his wife died about five years ago, and he never thought he would be interested in another woman. But when he saw Elia and heard her accent, he was fascinated. At first he thought the fascination was just the oddity of finding someone in northern New Mexico from his home village in Galicia. But when the fascination hung around, he began to wonder if it could lead to romance."

"And?"

She shrugged. "He'll be here for three weeks or so. Who knows what might happen? Look at us. After all these years, we're both finally married."

"Life is unpredictable."

"So you don't believe in determinism?"

"Not in general. But I do think there may sometimes be cases of predestination."

"Like what?"

"Like Abadias Minero."

"You think his death was predestined?"

"I do."

"Why?"

"Father Groaz told me about the real Solomon in the Bible. Groaz said The Book of Deuteronomy warns kings not to do three things: one, do not return to Egypt where Jews were mistreated; two, do not take too many wives; and three, do not accumulate large amounts gold. But King Solomon broke all three of those commands, and that's why God punished him in the end. Minero did the same thing as Solomon. He returned to Spain where Jews were mistreated during the Inquisition. He took too many wives. And he accumulated a lot of gold. And that's why he died."

She had a look of disbelief. "He had only one wife. Okay, let's say Elia was also a wife of sorts. But that's only two. Solomon had hundreds."

"You have to put it in the respective time frames. Solomon had five hundred wives when he should have limited himself to two hundred and fifty. He had twice as many as he should have had. But polygamy is illegal now, so two wives are twice as many as Abadias should have had. So he broke all three of those taboos."

She smiled at me. "Yep, seems like he was doomed. And when it's predestined, you really can't do anything about it. It's like Calvin said to Hobbes: 'Hobbes, some days even my lucky rocketship underpants don't help.'"

"John Calvin had rocketship underpants?"

"Calvin doesn't have a first name, Hubie. He's not John Calvin. He's just Calvin. Just like his friend is just Hobbes. No last names."

"Everybody has a last name."

"Not in comic strips."

"Comic strips?"

"I forgot. You don't read newspapers. Who did you think I was quoting and talking about?"

"I thought maybe it was John Calvin and Thomas Hobbes."

"You are so out-of-date."

I started to say something about John Calvin and Thomas Hobbes then thought better of it and said instead, "I am frequently out-of-date. But I like your modern quotes."

She raised her margarita and we clinked glasses.

Acknowledgments

The plotting of a book that deals with crypto-Judaism, four hundred years of New Mexico history, a dysfunctional family, characters who speak different dialects of Spanish (Castilian, Catalonian, Galician, Mexican, and Northern New Mexican), and three characters named Calvin was complicated.

For three months, the plot was a topic of discussion during my daily morning walks with my wife, Lai Chew Orenduff. I kept coming up with ideas, and she kept punching holes in them. And of course she was right. We were high school sweethearts. She was the valedictorian of our class; I was #75 out of 280 graduates.

As mentioned on the back cover of this book, she is a renowned author herself. She was a professor of art history and writes on that topic, but she enjoys reading fiction, and a large part of the success of the Pot Thief series is due to her involvement. The same can be said of my life.

About the Author

J. Michael Orenduff grew up in a house so close to the Rio Grande that he could Frisbee a tortilla into Mexico from his backyard. While studying for an MA at the University of New Mexico, he worked during the summer as a volunteer teacher at one of the nearby pueblos. After receiving a PhD from Tulane University, he became a professor. He went on to serve as president of New Mexico State University.

Orenduff took early retirement from higher education to write his award-winning Pot Thief murder mysteries, which combine archaeology and philosophy with humor and mystery. Among the author's many accolades are the Lefty Award for best humorous mystery, the Epic Award for best mystery or suspense ebook, and the New Mexico Book Award for best mystery or suspense fiction. His books have been described by the *Baltimore Sun* as "funny at a very high intellectual level" and "deliciously delightful," and by the *El Paso Times* as "the perfect fusion of murder, mayhem and margaritas."

THE POT THIEF MYSTERIES

FROM OPEN ROAD MEDIA

 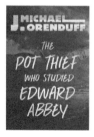 

OPEN ROAD

INTEGRATED MEDIA

Find a full list of our authors and
titles at www.openroadmedia.com

FOLLOW US
@OpenRoadMedia